The Yellow Hunter
Or, The Winding Trail of Death

by

T. C. Harbaugh

The Yellow Hunter
Or, The Winding Trail of Death

by T. C. Harbaugh

ISBN: 978-93-64287-90-6

Published by

DOUBLE 9 BOOKS

2/13-B, Ansari Road
Daryaganj, New Delhi – 110002
info@double9books.com
www.double9books.com
Tel. 011-40042856

ABOUT THE AUTHOR

T. C. Harbaugh The Stratemeyer Syndicate was a collection of writers who wrote a lot of dime books and series for kids and teens in the late 19th and early 20th century. They went by the pen name T. C. Harbaugh. Under the several pen names that the syndicate, headed by Edward Stratemeyer, used, it could produce stories fast. Though not much is known about the person who goes by the pseudonym T. C. Harbaugh, the name can be found on a number of dime novels, such as "The Girl Avenger or The Beautiful Terror of the Maumee." Because they satisfied the growing desire for exciting, action-packed fiction, these novels were well-liked in their day. Although T. C. Harbaugh's exact identity is still a mystery, his contributions to the dime book genre and the Stratemeyer Syndicate's larger body of work have had a long-lasting influence on American literature.

CONTENTS

CHAPTER I
BESIEGED

Pontiac, the Ottawa, was dead!

Yes, the fearless originator of the greatest Indian conspiracy on record had received a death-blow at the hands of a fellow red-man, and the promise of a barrel of English rum had nerved the villain's arm.

The bloody deed was committed in the forest of the Illinois, not far from Cahokia, on the Mississippi, and when the base-hearted Kaskaskia fled to his clansmen, with reeking hatchet, they sided with him, and, without a word in palliation of the crime, drove Pontiac's followers from the hamlet.

The great Ottawa's sachems spread over all the country, crying "blood for blood." They fired many a savage heart with the torch of vengeance, and inaugurated a war whose horrors stand without a parallel on the pages of American history.

From the bays and rivers that relieve the vast dreary western shore of Lake Michigan, rushed the Sacs, Foxes and Menomonies, to assist in the extirpation of the Illinois and the hated English who dwelt in the neighborhood where the conspirator was assassinated. Out from among the stately pines that cover that mighty peninsula between Huron and her western sister, came the intractable Ojibwa, the giant Ottawa, and the proverbially treacherous but brave Pottawatomie; and being joined on the Wabash by the Wyandots, the Miamies, and other more eastern tribes, they swooped down upon the Eden land that bordered the Father of Waters.

Their motto was, 'Death to the unprotected English and the Illinois Indians, but life to every Frenchman!'

Before the war that followed, all other Indian conflicts sink into utter insignificance, and over the grave of Pontiac more blood was poured out in atonement than flowed from the hecatombs of slaughtered heroes on the corpse of Patroclus:

And through the dark and bloody labyrinths of that era of death, the reader is about to follow the fortunes of red and white—fortunes which pale the cheek and almost turn the blood to ice.

"Father should have been here ere this. He said he would return at sunset. I wonder what keeps him. Surely no danger has befallen him. No, I know he can not be far away, and I will run toward the creek and meet him."

The speaker was a beautiful girl about eighteen years of age, and, as she uttered the last word, she bounded across the threshold of a low-browed cottage, and hurried toward the south.

She trailed a light rifle at her side, which, with her long, dark hair, and demi-Indian habiliments, gave her a decidedly romantic appearance. A few moments served to bring her to the stream, the Cahokia creek, which debouches into the lordly Mississippi a few miles above the ancient hamlet of like name. Pausing at the water's edge, she gazed far beyond the ford with anxious eyes.

The evening was a balmy one, in the early part of May, 1769, and the country of the Illinois wore robes of surpassing beauty. While not insensible to the delights of the landscape spread about her, Kate Blount continued to look for her father, who had taken a large bundle of furs to Cahokia, and had promised to return that evening.

Kate was not really fearful for her father's personal safety, but she knew his failing, and feared that an indulgence might detain him at the frontier station, and compel her to remain in their solitary cabin through a long night alone.

Of late, rumors of an approaching Indian war had reached the settlers in the Illinois, and many had already sought shelter in Cahokia and Fort Chartres. But, Oliver Blount had derided the stories of conflict, and declared that the avenging Indians would strike no one save the Illinois, and their fellow clansmen.

"They're going to extirpate the Illinois, root and branch," he would say, "but what have they to do with us? *We* didn't kill Pontiac!"

"But, father, English rum drove the tomahawk to the chief's brain," Kate had often replied, "and I tell you that more than one British scalp will hang at an Indian's belt when the carnage begins."

"Pooh! girl, that's all talk. You ain't as old as your father, who has no wish to show the white feather and hide behind Fort Chartres. No! we'll meet the war here!"

Poor, deluded Oliver Blount! He soon paid dearly for his stubbornness.

Kate felt that the war of extermination was near at hand, and, like a brave woman, prepared for it. During her father's journey to St. Louis and

Cahokia, she molded a store of bullets, and cleaned the little rifle which, a few weeks before the opening of our story, she had accepted from the hands of a young fur-trader, of whom, dear reader, more anon.

"I'm going to stay with father," she often murmured with determination, "and when he is in danger there will be one hand to save. Oh, I fear he will repent of his rashness when it is too late!"

For many minutes she watched the path leading from the ford; but the well-known form of the loved parent did not greet her eye, and at last, the young girl turned toward her home again.

"Father is tarrying before Kildare's bottles, I fear," she muttered, "and I— Hark! he is coming through the wood! He has missed the path."

Again she turned toward the stream, and a moment later, not her father, but an Indian, burst upon her sight!

Despite the shades now vailing the forest in gloom, she recognized him, when his feet touched the water at the ford.

"Swamp Oak!" she ejaculated, "and he has been chased, too, for I distinctly hear his pantings. Swamp Oak!"

She spoke the Indian's name in a louder tone, when, with a light cry of recognition he plunged into the water.

A minute brought him to the girl's side, and he cast his eyes over his shoulder before he allowed her to address him. Then he turned to her with a significant look which told her that the danger was passed, and that he awaited her pleasure.

"Where did the Swamp Oak come from?" questioned Kate Blount, eagerly.

"From the stone-walled fort," was the quick reply.

The young Peoria could speak good English.

"Did you see my father?"

"No; the white trader's shadow fell not across Swamp Oak's trail. He made many a leaf bleed, Lone Dove."

A faint smile wreathed the boy's lips as he spoke the last sentence.

"You've been tracked, then?" said Kate Blount.

"The Ojibwa wolves were on the Peoria's trail," answered the youth; "but he proved too swift for them, and in the great forest they lost him."

"Then the hatchet has been unearthed?"

"Yes, yes," cried the Indian. "Between Cahokia and the stone-walled fort the enemies of the Illinois outnumber the leaves of the trees. The Ojibwa has sunk his boat, and now seeks red and white scalps: the—"

"Not white scalps, Swamp Oak?"

"White scalps, Lone Dove! Swamp Oak run by a pale-face's cabin, and he saw a white maiden dead by the well."

Kate Blount shuddered and thought of her father.

"Swamp Oak's people must die!" continued the young chief, sadly; "but they will die like their fathers died. But, Lone Dove, we must not stand here, and for three days Swamp Oak has lived on roots."

With a last anxious look across the stream, the young woman turned toward her home again, the brave walking at her side.

"I saw him, White Flower," he said, suddenly.

Kate Blount started at the announcement, and a crimson flush suffused her beautiful cheeks.

"And when is he coming?" she asked, when she regained her composure.

"Even now he is on the way," was the reply. "He sent Swamp Oak before, and he and the Pale Giant will be here after another sleep."

"Not before?" asked Kate, with a sigh.

"If they are chased—yes," answered the Indian.

"Then may they be chased!" she ejaculated, inaudibly, and a moment later the barking of a dog told the twain that they were near the frontier cottage.

I have used the word cottage simply for the reason that the house of Oliver Blount was not a cabin, but in reality a cottage. It was the work of the hands of a former owner—a proud Frenchman, who left the Illinois paradise when the English flag supplanted the *fleur de lis*, after the peace of 1763; and for a nominal sum Oliver Blount purchased the building, when he reached Cahokia, in the rear of the British army of occupation. The cottage was quite small, but picturesque in the extreme. It contained three rooms, two on the ground floor, and one, a roomy attic, beneath the strong clapboard roof. It boasted of broad eaves, covered with climbers, and a pretty veranda, swarming with flowers, planted in deep wooden bowls.

The young Peoria was not a stranger at the Blounts' home, for when the giant bulldog saw him he ceased his barkings, and greeted the red-skin with a low, joyful whine. Kate entered the house and began to prepare an evening repast, while the Peoria leaned against the door and swept the landscape before him with his eagle eye. Night had fairly vailed the earth now; but the Indian did not desert his position. His eyes seemed to penetrate the gloom far beyond the threshold, and when he uttered an expressive "ugh," Kate sprung to him and touched his arm.

"Father?"

"No!" exclaimed Swamp Oak, and the next moment he stepped back and gently closed the strong oaken door.

Then he calmly proceeded to barricade it, Kate watching his movements without a question.

When he deemed the portal proof against the foe, he turned to the windows and secured them in like manner.

"Lone Dove, the wolves prowl about your nest," he said at last, pausing directly before Kate, "and ere long their steps will greet your ears."

He had scarcely paused when a footfall approached the house, and fell heavily upon the ashen floor of the veranda. It was greeted by a growl from the dog, who approached the door with all his furious passions aroused, and with fire flashing from his great gray eyes.

The next moment Kate darted forward and quieted Pontiac with her hand, while the Peoria placed his ear at the foot of the portal to catch the import of the whispers on the porch.

All at once, while the Indian still remained crouched on the floor, a hand struck the door, and in a firm tone Kate Blount demanded to know who was there.

"Segowatha, the war-wolf of the Pottawatomies, knocks at the pale-face's lodge," was the reply, in a pompous tone. "He is not alone; his warriors are about him, and through him they command the Englishman's daughter to deliver over to them the Peoria dog, who kennels beneath her roof. We have tracked the Swamp Oak hither, and we seek the scalp of the Peoria dog, and not the Lone Dove's. Let the pale child be swift to speak, for Segowatha's warriors are impatient, and soon he can not hold them back from the work of the evil spirit."

Silence followed the chief's words. While he spoke, the hunted Peoria had risen to his feet, and now he stood with bowed head before the girl who held his life in her hands. Kate Blount gazed upon the demanded sacrifice, and twice she essayed to speak, but in vain. In the form of the young Peoria she beheld the only true red friend she ever had, and now to deliver him up to the torture seemed to her simple mind the hight of ingratitude.

"Speak, Lone Dove," suddenly cried Segowatha, and he supplemented the command with a blow from his hatchet. "My warriors are drawing their weapons!"

"Let them draw and use them if they wish," cried Kate Blount, starling toward the door. "I refuse to deliver the Peoria to his hunters, and more, I shall defend him with my own life."

A yell of rage burst from the Pottawatomie's throat, and he drove his tomahawk into the door.

That blow caused Swamp Oak to spring erect as an arrow, and he griped the slender arm of the trader's daughter.

"Swamp Oak will die for the Lone Dove!" he said, with mingled determination and emotion. "Segowatha is full of lies. They seek the pale girl as well as Swamp Oak, for she is English, and in this war they strike all save the French. A yellow-skinned dog is with Segowatha; he wants the dove with golden plumage; he— Ah! the dog is going to whine."

The Peoria's sentence was broken by a voice just beyond the threshold, and the twain grew silent to hear what it might say.

"White girl, you are rash," said the invisible speaker, in French. "You are selling your life for a dog's. The Indians don't want you—only the Peoria lout."

"No more, Jules Bardue!" cried Kate Blount, with flashing eyes. "I know you; you can't disguise your hated voice. I know what brought you hither, and death is far preferable to the life you have marked out for me. Depart immediately, base creole dog, else, through this door, a bullet shall stop your whinings."

A terrible anathema burst from the lips of the maddened creole, and there was a hasty flight from the porch.

"Ha, they run!" cried Kate, turning to the Peoria.

"But they will come again," was the reply. "The Yellow Chief will have the Lone Dove or die!"

The lips of the trader's daughter met in terrible determination, and a low whine from Pontiac announced the return of the savages.

A moment later a heavy blow fell upon the door; but the barricades resisted to good effect, and, throwing down the battering-ram, the savages poured a volley of musket-balls through the planks. Suspecting their design, our friends had taken shelter behind the heavy logs that nestled behind the plank weather-boarding, and thus escaped the leaden pellets. Scarcely had the balls perforated the door, when Swamp Oak sprung to his feet and fired through the protection.

A death-yell, similar to the yelp of the wolf, announced the result of his shot, and a moment later Kate Blount's rifle sent an Ottawa to the hunting-grounds of his tribe.

The lucky shots drew a chorus of demoniac yells from the savages, and while the brave twain reloaded their weapons, those outside rushed in a body against the door.

The first blow with the sapling which they had deserted a moment before, sent a shiver over the structure, and the second stroke drove the faithful door from its hinges!

The ram was handled by demons now, and nothing could resist their fury.

The broken barricades prevented the door from falling to the floor, but the moonlight streamed into the room, and revealed the defenders to the Indians. Simultaneously with their success, they essayed to enter over the stricken portals, but the rifles of the besieged cracked again, and two more Indians fell dead on the porch.

The death-work momentarily drove the foe from the door, and before they returned to their work, Swamp Oak had torn the useless barricades away, and supplied their places with new ones. A settler's cabin is always supplied with two sets of barricades, and in case of an attack the extra set is placed beside the door.

When the enemy returned to the attack, they greeted the new defense with wild yells, and the renewal of the attack was met with a volley from the besieged which sorely wounded no less a personage than Segowatha.

In tones of rage and pain the stricken Pottawatomie ordered his braves from the attack, and for many minutes silence reigned beyond the fort.

"They are concocting something devilish," whispered the young girl.

"Yes, the evil spirit is playing with their hearts," said Swamp Oak.

A moment later, they heard the voice of the Yellow Chief.

"You had better surrender; the Indians are mad now," he said.

"Let them eat themselves for rage," cried Kate Blount, heroically. "We will not surrender."

"Then die!" yelled Jules Bardue.

A moment later innumerable sticks were hurled upon the porch.

In the moonlight that stole into the room through a crevice above the window, the eyes of the red brave and white girl met.

"They're going to burn us out!" said Kate.

The Peoria nodded assent, griped his rifle more firmly than ever, and stepped to the door.

The next instant the clash of flints greeted his ears. Kate heard it, too.

CHAPTER II
DEATH'S DOINGS

The brushwood which the Indians heaped against the door of Oliver Blount's home, had been gathered on the edge of the clearing and was quite dry. The bark films were soon ignited by the flints, and in less time than we can record a single sentence, the little boughs were cracking in the ruddy blaze.

Segowatha, who, on account of his wound, lay at the foot of a tree some distance from the cottage, commanded his braves to draw back from the scene, and with a single exception they obeyed. That exception was Jules Bardue, the Yellow Chief, as he had been termed for several years. He had suddenly disappeared, though Segowatha made no inquiries regarding his absence, nor manifested any uneasiness about it.

The creole was a privileged character among the north-western Indians. He had not always dwelt among the tribes of the Illinois country. He had been an attache to Sir William Johnson's estate in New York, and amid its beauties he first encountered the girl he now sought—Catherine Blount. Then she was a pretty little blonde of fifteen, and he a manly-looking fellow of one and twenty. He threw himself before Miss Kate whenever an opportunity presented, and when he discovered that the beauty did not love him—when, in indignant tones, she bade him remain from her side, he obeyed the instincts of a bad heart and grossly insulted her.

As young as she was—a mere child in years—Kate Blount had imbibed to no little degree her father's resentful nature, and it was with great difficulty that the creole wrenched from her the pistol which had flashed from her bosom to avenge the insult he had offered.

To what violence his passion might have led we can only guess, for from among the shadows of the forest trees a veritable giant sprung upon him; strong arms encircled him, and, before he could think with calmness, he found himself stripped and bound to a tree. Kate Blount had suddenly disappeared, and before him stood her irate father, armed with a bundle of switches. Jules Bardue did not beg for mercy; he was not that kind of a man.

On the contrary he gritted his teeth until sixty terrible blows had stripped the flesh from his back, and he was unbound and hurled almost senseless to the ground.

The next morning the creole, or Frenchman as he was called by many, did not make his appearance at Sir William's lodge; nor was he ever seen near it again. He feared the wrath of Oliver Blount, and had left the country for his own and the country's good.

He fled to the new Illinois; lived at Cahokia awhile, then joined the Pottawatomies, and became their Yellow Chief. He knew that Oliver Blount intended to emigrate to the Illinois country sometime, and the Yellow Chief's frequent incursions into that Paradise told that he watched and waited for father and daughter—for his revenge.

Fully thirty paces from trader Blount's cottage the Indians watched the progress of their devilish work, and when they beheld the flames licking up the door with their forked tongues, they exchanged "ughs" of supreme satisfaction. The besieged would not permit themselves to be roasted to death, and every minute the dusky demons expected to hear the submissive cry. A cordon of braves encircled the cottage thus cutting off the retreat of the doomed ones.

But while this was transpiring, a merciful Providence was interposing a saving hand, for a suddenly-gathered storm-cloud burst over the cottage; the gates of the upper deep opened, and threatened to deluge every thing.

The superstitious Indians, surprised and alarmed at this sudden burst of lightning and rain, left their stations and gathered around the wounded chief.

Despite his wounds, Segowatha sprung to his feet.

"Back to your places, braves!" he yelled, facing the shrinking savages with drawn tomahawk. "The Manitou merely waters the earth, and he will smile soon."

Sullenly the warriors returned to their posts, and again the cottage was encircled by the tomahawk and scalping-knife.

The drenching rain, driven in upon the porch by the wind, effectually extinguished the flames; and when the storm at last had subsided, an Indian approached the house, to discover a door so charred that it must yield to a slight assault.

Not a sound proceeded from the cottage, and the Indians, who now crept forward like snakes to the attack, wondered at the silence. When they reached the foot of the porch they rose in a body and threw themselves against the door.

It made no resistance, and the savages, with horrible yells, rushed pell-mell into the cottage. Beyond the portal they met a determined resistance, but it was from a dog. With an almost human yell, Pontiac darted at the foremost Indian's throat, and dragged the torn wretch to the floor. The entire band sprung upon the dog, and a minute later he was literally hacked to pieces with their knives.

Where were Kate Blount and the hunted Peoria?

The savages rushed into the second chamber; but it was tenantless. The ladder which was wont to invite ingress to the attic was missing, and with some difficulty the red demons gained the upper story. A moment later a yell of mingled rage and disappointment pealed from their throats, and while it echoed throughout the gloomy recesses of the drenched forest, they congregated beneath an opening in the roof, and gazed bewildered at the stars which seem to laugh at their defeat.

The birds had flown!

Segowatha greeted this announcement with a groan of rage, and in angry tones he summoned the rear guards into his presence. Tremblingly they approached, and told him that while they guarded the house, the twain had not escaped.

"But while you acted like squaws they crept from the lodge," cried the War Wolf with terrific mien. "I will have no such braves with me!"

As he spoke he buried his hatchet in the brain of the foremost guard, and turned with murderous intention upon the second. But, his strength failed him; the weapon dropped from his hand, and a sub-chief supported him with his arms.

"Shall we throw ourselves upon the snake's trail?"

"No, no!" said Segowatha, his face suddenly growing pale, and a convulsive shudder passing over his giant frame. "The War Wolf must go to his people; the Peoria's bullet struck deep. Segowatha is near the dark river. But give the snake's den to the fire, and call the Yellow Chief back."

With the bare thought of their war-chief's approaching end, the savages gave themselves over to a rage which knew no bounds, and defies description.

They flew to the work of destruction; they ripped the weather boarding from the cottage, and split it with their hatchets, piling it in the lower rooms. Presently the flints were applied again, and soon Oliver Blount's home was wrapped in flames. While the tongues of fire licked up the toil of years, a chief repeated the shrill cry of the night-hawk three times in rapid succession. Then they waited anxiously for the coming of some one, but, whoever that one was, he did not come.

The demons danced about the trader's burning home; they tore down the neat fence that surrounded it, and cast it into the fire; they applied their hatchets to the beautiful silver maples which afforded delicious shade, and gave them to the devouring element. In short, they spared nothing, even tearing up the broad stones which led to the well, and hurling them with terrible yells after the trees.

At last the cottage was destroyed, and, ready for more hellish work, the Indians turned to Segowatha for orders. The dying chief, for it was plain that he was approaching the river of death, smiled upon their work and inquired regarding the creole.

"He comes not," answered a young chief—the Lone Wolf, "like a cowardly dog he has deserted us. We will whip him with canes when he sneaks back to our lodges."

"The Yellow Chief went to watch the spot where the fur-trader keeps his boat," said Segowatha. "But Segowatha can not dream why he comes not. He must have heard the hawk cry."

"He may have filled his ears with leaves," said Lone Wolf, who, though a Pottawatomie, bore no good thoughts for Jules Bardue. "He watches yet, perhaps. We will hunt the dog."

Touching a warrior's arm lightly, the young Indian bounded toward Cahokia Creek, followed by the red-skin whom his touch had summoned.

A path led from the cottage to the creek, which almost encircled it, and the two Indians were not long in reaching the stream. Suddenly Lone Wolf's companion uttered an "ugh" expressive of horror, and dropped before a dark object which lay near the water.

"The Yellow Chief!" exclaimed Lone Wolf.

A brief examination proved the creole to be still living, and just recovering from the deathly swoon into which a terrible blow had hurled him.

A glance about the star-lit spot showed evidences of a fierce struggle, and the missing boat told the result of the combat.

The Indians lifted the Yellow Chief and bore him to Segowatha.

The War Wolf raised himself on his elbow, and for a long time looked down into the creole's face without speaking.

"Segowatha leads the red-men of the big lake no more," he said, at last, in the calmest of tones, which the Indian loves to assume when he stands upon the threshold of death. "The Manitou grips his hand now, and the War Wolf must go. Warriors—Pottawatomies, Ojibwas," his eyes swept the circle of tawny faces, "who followed Segowatha hither, you must swear."

In the momentary pause that followed, thirty hatchets flew aloft, and thirty hands covered the hearts of their respective owners.

"Swear!" cried the dying War Wolf—"swear to hunt to earth the Peoria skunk and the white house-snake who crawls after him. Swear to tear the hearts from all whom she loves—her bearded father, the Pale Giant, and the boy with long hair. Segowatha hates them all!"

"We swear!" cried Lone Wolf. "Warriors, by our chieftain's blood we swear all this."

With the last word the young brave dyed his hands in the warm blood that gushed afresh from Segowatha's wounds, and the other red-skins followed his example.

"I swear, too!" unexpectedly cried a voice in French, and, raising himself with a mighty effort, the Yellow Chief thrust his hand into Segowatha's blood. "Ha! ha! we will hunt them down—the fugitives of the Illinois! Oh, that they were here now!"

Exhaustion then again followed, and he dropped to the ground, and a moment later a terrific yell, uttered simultaneously by thirty pair of lips, told that the mighty War Wolf of the Pottawatomies had stepped into the impenetrable future.

Over Segowatha's corpse an Ojibwa dropped with a groan, and two others staggered to their feet to fall to the earth, a second later, wounded to the death.

The uninjured red-skins griped their rifles; but not a foe was to be seen. Everywhere the silence of death reigned supreme!

CHAPTER III
A MOTHER'S VENGEANCE

From a trap-door in the roof of the cottage, Swamp Oak, the young Peoria, had noted the approach of the delivering storm, and had hastened to communicate the joyful tidings to his beautiful fellow-prisoner. Well understanding the nature of the summer storms which broke over the forests of the Illinois, they were alert at once, and when the cloud did discharge its fury of wind and rain through the Stygian darkness, they were in the attic, and by the flashes of lightning, saw the awe-stricken guards desert their posts, just as the Peoria knew they would do.

The young red-skin then glided away to the edge of the broad eaves, followed by the girl, whom he lowered to the ground. Handing her the rifles, he sprung down. Then toward the trader's boat the fugitives of the Illinois hurried.

Suddenly, when they were very near the creek, the Peoria paused, and griped Kate Blount's arm.

"What is it, Swamp Oak?" questioned the girl, in a low whisper.

"The Yellow Chief," was the reply, and then the Indian left her standing alone.

A flash of lightning had revealed to Swamp Oak the figure of the creole chief watching the boat, as though he were certain that the besieged would escape, in which event they would, of course, seek the boat.

Several minutes of silence followed the Peoria's departure, and then the sounds of a desperate struggle were borne to the girl's ears. In the gloom she stood and trembled for the safety of her ally, and when at last the lightning revealed the two men locked in each other's arms, writhing and twisting like two panthers on the verge of Cahokia Creek, she sprung forward to put an end to the conflict. The electric light had told her that the Yellow Chief was uppermost, and Swamp Oak's situation critical in the extreme.

A few bounds brought her to the spot; her rifle flew above her head to deal a death-blow to the coward who sought to destroy her happiness, when she saw him roll from the Indian and lie perfectly still on the bank.

"Ugh!" grunted the victorious Peoria, springing to his feet, and shaking himself after the manner of a dog emerging from the water. "The Yellow Chief is as strong as the buffalo; but he was no match for Swamp Oak.

"Come!" he said, stepping to the water, "we must fly, even as the wild geese fly from the gun of the white hunters."

"But father and the others?" said Kate, involuntarily pausing beside the boat.

"They will come to the Lone Dove in time," said the Swamp Oak; "she will nestle in her father's bosom soon, and she will plait the young trader's long hair before the death of another moon. Come!"

Thus reassured, Kate Blount stepped into the boat, and the next moment they were flying toward the head-waters of Cahokia creek.

"Why did you not fly to the fort, chief?" asked Kate, after a lengthy silence.

"The Red Avengers were between the fur man's cabin and the English flag; and we must keep from them. Oh, my poor people!" and a sigh escaped the Indian's breast. "Swamp Oak's father is old; the evil spirits' fiery arrows shoot along his bones, and like the wounded dove, he will fall an easy prey to the bad Indians' tomahawks. But let them kill him," and the young brave gritted his teeth; "yes, let them kill the old Peoria, and they shall unchain a devil fiercer than all the wolves in the country of the Illinois."

Then the savage relapsed into silence, which was not broken till, an hour later, he ran the canoe to the secure cover of the fringed bank.

"Now where do we go, Swamp Oak?" demanded Kate, as they stepped upon the bank.

"The Lone Dove shall see," answered the Indian, with a smile. "Did she never know that Swamp Oak had a squaw?"

"No, chief," said the girl, in astonishment. "You never breathed a word to me about a Mrs. Swamp Oak."

The youthful Indian smiled sadly, but proudly, and, having sunk the boat, led the way into the forest.

"Yes," he said, in low tones, while he guided the trader's daughter over the rough ground, "the Peoria has a squaw, as beautiful as the lilies of snow that kiss the lips of the great river (Mississippi). Many moons ago, Swamp Oak's nation sent him to the lands of the Delawares to spy. He went with a fearless heart, for he wanted to win his first feathers. He wore the plumes and paint of an Ojibwa; he entered the lodges of the Delawares; he told them about the great lake where the Ojibwas live, and they believed him, for the Manitou closed their eyes to the fact that Swamp Oak was an Illinois. [1] Among the Delaware wigwams he met Ulalah, the daughter of Colealah, the gigantic Delaware prophetess, who wears a necklace of living snakes. He loved her star eyes, and when he left the Delawares, Ulalah walked at his side. He dared not take her to his people as his squaw—she a hated and accursed Delaware, so he brought her—here!"

The young white girl looked up into the Indian's face, bewildered.

"Not here, Swamp Oak?"

"Here, Lone Dove."

As the savage finished, he stooped and placed his ear to the ground. In this position he remained for some time, when, satisfied with his vigil, he stepped to a gigantic oak and thrust his arm into a dark aperture in its side.

Kate Blount watched him eagerly.

When Swamp Oak withdrew his arm, a portion of the tree swung open like a door, which unexpected action drew a cry of astonishment from the girl's lips.

"So Swamp Oak and his squaw live in a tree?" she said, smiling at the novelty of the thought.

"No," murmured the Indian, "they dwell below the tree. Come!"

He caught Kate's arm and led her beyond the living threshold of his strange home; and she stood against the inner wall of the tree, while he closed the door and made it secure again.

Then he gently assisted her down a ladder formed of poles and sinews, and at last Kate found herself upon firm, stony ground, thirty feet below the roots of the tree.

In the gloom the Peoria paused, and a loud bird-call pealed from his lips.

It received no answer. He called again, and in the suspense that followed the cry, Kate felt a shudder flit over the red-skin's tawny frame.

"Ulalah must sleep," said Swamp Oak, in a tone full of uncertainty and fears. "Swamp Oak has not kissed her for ten sleeps, and she has grown weary waiting for him. We will awake her, Lone Dove. Come!"

The hand that stole to Kate Blount's in the gloom trembled like the aspen, and a terrible presentiment of evil crept to her young heart. She could not shake the terror off, and she knew that Swamp Oak shared it with her.

"Ha!" suddenly exclaimed the Indian, in a somewhat joyous tone, "Ulalah still keeps the fire bright for Swamp Oak."

He quickened his gait now, and presently the turning of a curve brought them into an apartment quite vividly relieved by a fire that burned in the center.

The chamber was fit for the banquet hall of an eastern king, and the trader's daughter was struck with rapture and awe when her eyes fell upon the myriads of shining stalactites that hung pendent from the arched ceiling, and the walls that reflected back, with ten thousand beauties, the glow of the fire.

At first she thought the palace deserted; but when her eyes became accustomed to the light, she, simultaneously with the Peoria, beheld a figure upon a mat of doe skins, near the bright blaze.

With a light cry of "Ulalah!" Swamp Oak shot forward, and stooped, with his inborn gentleness, over the motionless body of his young wife.

But the next moment he started back with a cry that drove every vestige of color from Kate Blount's face, and, with the eyes of a madman, he stared at the form on the doe-skins.

The trader's daughter could not move. Horror glued her to the spot, and her eyes continually flitted between the mad Peoria and his Ulalah.

Suddenly Swamp Oak shot forward, and lifted the Delaware girl from the couch, and then without a word bore her to the trader's child, and thrust the cold, expressionless face into hers.

"Dead! dead!" welled from Kate's lips, in horrible accents, and while she spoke she could scarcely believe that the beautiful being embraced by the Indian was a corpse.

"Dead! dead!" shrieked Swamp Oak echoing the girl's words with a voice that was a wail; and while the accents still quivered on his pale lips, he staggered back and dropped Ulalah upon the couch again.

"He's mad!" muttered Kate Blount, involuntarily shrinking from the intense glare of the frenzied Indian's eyes. "This deed of blood has sent reason from its throne. What is to follow God knows. Heaven protect me!"

The Peoria approached with an unnatural smile.

"Yes, the good spirits have taken Ulalah to their lodges," he said, "and left the Lone Dove to be poor Swamp Oak's squaw. Swamp Oak loved

Ulalah; but when the winged spirits came for her, he kissed her, and let her go. Ha! ha! ha! the Lone Dove will be lone no longer. Why does she not greet the Swamp Oak? Come, we'll strew the bridal-couch with flowers."

But, with a shudder, Kate continued to retreat, and when at last, unable to retreat further, the demented Indian's hand griped her arm, a fiendishly triumphant laugh came from a distant portion of the cave.

Instantly Swamp Oak dropped her arm, and wheeled with a crazy cry.

He turned in time to see a giantess burst from one of the corridors, leading from the further end of the chamber, and Kate Blount echoed the Indian's cry of horror.

She at once recognized in the red ogress, the person of Coleola the prophetess of the Delawares, for around her neck writhed three snakes, pictures of horror.

Several warriors followed the red queen, and she threw a furtive glance upon Ulalah's corpse as she sprung forward.

"Ha! ha! ha!" she laughed again, more discordantly than ever, pausing within a few feet of Swamp Oak, who regarded her with an expression utterly indescribable. "At last Coleola has tracked the child-stealer to his den. At last she has found her child—found her to punish her for following the Peoria dog into the woods. See!" and a knife flashed from beneath her tunic, "this blade is red with the blood of the ungrateful girl, and soon it shall drink the heart-gore of the red hound. For five sleeps we have waited for Swamp Oak, the traitor. Coleola led her braves from the Delaware village, saying: 'We dye our knives in the hearts of the runaways or never return.' Ha! ha! in the forest we saw a pair of eyes peeping from a tree! Ulalah watched for her red dog, and Coleola came instead of he."

Again that hellish laugh broke from the murderess' lips, and with eyes aflame with passion, she strode toward Swamp Oak, who did not seem to comprehend her intention. Kate Blount, still griping her rifle, shrunk nearer the wall, determined to brace herself against it, and sell her life as dearly as possible. While Coleola addressed Swamp Oak, her eyes had wandered to her, and Kate knew that she was doomed to die by some terrible mode of death.

Nearer and nearer the dazed Indian came the murderess, and her almost naked followers; when to Kate Blount's surprise, Swamp Oak, with a terrific yell, dashed Coleola and her braves from his path as though they were stalks of corn; and, snatching up the corpse of his stolen wife, he disappeared in one of the corridors before the astonished spectators had recovered from their confusion.

Coleola and her followers darted after the madman, and Kate Blount was left alone. Then, with the instinct of self-preservation, she retreated back through the passage which a few minutes since she had traversed, and at last found herself in the tree. Around her all was gloom, and she fumbled about for the fastenings with the wildest heart that ever throbbed in maiden's bosom.

Every moment was precious to her, and when she at last found the sinews and threw wide the door, she felt a foot on the ladder below!

She sprung from the tree into the day that was penetrating the Illinois forest, and heard the triumphant yell of the Indian behind her.

Impelled by her danger, she turned and beheld, rushing from the tree with uplifted hatchet, one of Coleola's braves.

Instantly her rifle shot to her shoulder; she touched the trigger and the Delaware lay motionless on the leaves with a bullet in his brain!

Again, with a prayer to God for safety, the fugitive turned and rushed toward Cahokia Creek, loading her faithful rifle as she ran.

From childhood the trader's daughter handled the weapons of the frontier, and about Sir William Johnson's "lodge" there used to be no deadlier shot than the then little girl of fifteen!

In her hands the rifle was a dangerous thing!

[1] The Kaskaskias, Peorias and Cahokias were component tribes of the Illinois nation.

CHAPTER IV
THE HAUNTED TRADER

"Shall we give the red-livered dogs another volley?"

The questioner was a youth, apparently twenty years of age, and the looks which he threw upon the startled Indians was burdened with the consuming fire of hatred.

"No, Rob," was the whispered rejoiner of a herculean man who lay behind the log at the young scout's side. "Another volley would bring the hull ov the red devils down upon us before we could reload, an' then thar'd be the very Old Harry to pay. They'll not hunt for us as it is; they're pickin' up their dead now, an' ar' goin' to break fur Cahokia. Wonder who dropped Segowatha?"

"And I wonder where my daughter—my Kate—is?"

It was Oliver Blount that spoke, and his face told of the fearful anxiety and doubting that gnawed at his heart. He was enduring the greatest anguish that can assail a father's breast for the fate of his only child.

"The Lord only knows where she is, Oll," responded the giant, in a sympathizing tone; "and, b'lieve me, He's goin' to take care o' her until you see her again."

A ray of hope lighted up Blount's eyes, and he grasped Doc Bell's hand.

"Then you think her living, Doc?"

"Why, in course she's alive," said the hunter and Indian-fighter, confidently. "Ef them red devils had cotched her, why she'd be with 'em now; but, you see, the only live thing they found in yer house war Pontiac, an' I'll bet my rifle that he let out some red hound's blood afore he yelped fur the last time. Ha! jest as I told ye; they're goin'."

A smile played with the giant's face as he saw the savages lift their dead from the ground, and move toward Cahokia Creek.

"Look yonder!" suddenly exclaimed Oliver Blount, his eyes riveted upon the Yellow Chief, who, with the assistance of two Miamis, regained his feet. "I know who the Yellow Chief is now—Jules Bardue."

"That's jest his name!" said Bell, "an' a devil he is, too. Yer daughter did good work to-night, Oll, but she ought to hev finished the Creole."

"But he will die," said Rob Somerville, the young scout. "Look at his face; death is riding over it now."

"No, he ain't, boy," said the giant. "To kill Jules Bardue you must send a bullet to his brain. I'll never forget the night, near two years ago, when I met him near the 'Wattomie town, and hacked him to pieces with my knife. I made that scar over his left eye; I cut the thumb from his left hand, an' four times I drove my blade between the scoundrel's ribs. I left him for dead. I piled brush over 'im, an' ran like oiled lightnin'. But as I live! a month arterwards I saw the Yellow Chief on Lake Michigan. Somehow or other he had come to life, an' doctored himself up in the latest style. But, boys, the next time I'll finish 'im; thar's no remedy, you know, fur a bullet in the brain."

When the hunter concluded, the savages were beyond sight, and after scouring the woods to see that none remained behind, the trio approached the blasted sight of Oliver Blount's home.

"They shall pay for this!" hissed the fur-trader, through clenched teeth, and then he stopped before a ghastly object—the body of his faithful dog.

While he bent over it, stroking the bloody hair with the air and look of a grief-stricken man, the giant and his youthful protege returned from a scout around the cottage.

"Yer daughter is safe, Oll," said Bell.

The trader started at the sound of the voice, for the two men had stolen up behind him.

"How do you know she's safe?" he demanded.

"Because your boat is gone, an' she an' that young Peoria ar' in it."

"Gone down Cahokia right into the jaws of death."

"Not much. Swamp Oak ain't a durned fool if he is young. He's gone up Cahokia, to his mysterious home."

"Do you know where it is?" and Oliver Blount griped the hunter's arm in his eagerness.

"Not exactly, but I kin tramp mighty nigh it. Ye see, that young red chap stole his wife, an' he won't tell anybody whar he keeps her. But we'll hunt for the place, an' we'll begin right away. I'd give any thing fur a boat now."

But no canoe was to be had, and the trio were obliged to set out on the hunt for Kate Blount on foot.

They had arrived too late to attack the Indians while they besieged the devoted pair in the cottage; but they reached the spot from whence they slew the three red-men in time to hear the oath which Segowatha imposed upon his followers.

Doc Bell and young Somerville had lately left Fort Chartres for the purpose of conducting the Blount family to a place of safety, or to defend them should the father still persist in his refusal to move. To warn the trader of his danger, and to tell him that they would soon be with him, they had dispatched Swamp Oak, the Peoria, before them; and, as the reader has seen, the Indian reached the doomed cottage in time to render valuable assistance to its beautiful tenant.

A short distance from Fort Chartres the twain encountered Indians, and accidentally ran across a young Delaware brave, with whom a meeting, in his own country, some years prior to the date of our romance, had placed Bell on friendly terms. The Delaware told them of the presence of the avengers; that that night the blow was to be struck, and that the home of every backwoods English settler would be in ashes before dawn.

This startling intelligence impelled our two friends forward faster than ever, and when they struck the trail leading from Cahokia to the trader's house, they encountered Oliver flying to the protection of his loved daughter. He had been detained in Cahokia beyond his time, and he had much to relate about the bursting of the storm of massacre. His path had been illuminated by the light of happy homes, and he had had several narrow escapes while on his homeward journey.

From the destroyed cottage the trio proceeded to the scene of the struggle between Swamp Oak and the Yellow Chief; and, with Doc Bell in advance, struck up the creek.

"I tell you what," said the giant, "we're in an uncommon delicate pickle jest now. Thar's a wall ov red meat all around us, an' unless we kin break through it, the circle will narrow down to a point so fine as to be extremely disagreeable."

"But, with Kate, we're going to break through it!" said Blount, with determination.

"That's jest what's the matter," responded the hunter. "The red devils may surround me in a ten-acre woods, an' ef I don't get out all right, they may marry me to the ugliest squaw they've got. Bob an' me's been in tight places afore."

"And so have I," said Blount; "and we're going to get out of this. But we'll be hunted like deers. When the Red Avengers deliver Segowatha to the rest of the tribe, they'll return and hunt us down."

"You're right thar, Blount, an' ef they catch any ov us they'll sarve us like they sarved poor John Senior, on the shores of Huron."

"How was that?" asked Blount.

"They made him eat his ears, an' then, with dull knives, they skinned him alive."

Despite his manhood, Oliver Blount shuddered.

"I saw that done," continued Bell, "an' the hellion who proposed it swore this night to hunt us down."

"I know who you mean—Jules Bardue."

"Yes, it was he."

The thought of 'Jack' Senior's fate, and their own peril caused the trio to drop the unpalatable conversation, and for a long time they skirted the shores of Cahokia creek in silence. Far above them the stars twinkled with a dimmed luster, as if they were sorrowing for the work falling from the hands of the demon Devastation, stalking over the Eden land of the Illinois.

Oliver Blount walked along with bowed head—repenting, when too late, of his stubbornness. Had he listened to reason at that hour he and his daughter might have been safe behind the protecting walls of Fort Chartres; but now she was a fugitive from Indian vengeance, and he rushing to death in the attempt to save her young life. He trusted to his more watchful companions to warn him of the presence of foes, and suddenly that warning came in the click of their rifles.

"What is it?" he asked in a whisper.

"Down!" returned the giant.

They crouched in the weeds that lined the bank of the little stream, and the footsteps of a single person approached them from the recesses of the forest.

"He's making for the creek," whispered Somerville. "If an Indian, we'll finish him."

"It's a pale-face," said Bell. "Listen again, Bob. Does he run like an Injun?"

The young man did not reply, and presently the new-comer crossed an open spot in which the trio caught a glimpse of his figure. He was a tall man, clad in the garb of the English fur trader, and bore a long rifle at his side. His haggard face told of a terror-stricken heart; and it was not difficult for the trio to tell that he was flying from the blood-dyed tomahawk of Pontiac's avengers.

He paused on the bank of the stream, and resting his sharply defined chin upon his shoulder, listened for the footsteps of his pursuers.

The three hunters could almost have touched him with their gun-barrels.

They watched him narrowly, and when he seemed about to plunge into the stream, and break his trail by water, Doc Bell spoke:

"Williamson?"

The hunted man started, and a low cry of despair parted his ashen lips. Our friends heard the click, click of his long weapon, and his fiery, blood-shot eyes seemed to pierce their covert.

"Come on!" he hissed. "John Williamson never surrenders. For three weeks I've been the most wretched man on earth. Awake or asleep, I've been hunted by the ghost of that mighty chief whose life I purchased for a barrel of rum. I want to die, and now come on, and let me take to Hades with me a dozen red demons."

"We don't want your life, John Williamson, though I could take it without a guilty conscience," said Oliver Blount, who recognized the man who had precipitated the bloody war upon the country, by compassing the death of the great conspirator, Pontiac.

The haunted trader recognized Blount's voice, and a moment later he stood before the three men.

"Will you not save me?" he pleaded, suddenly discovering that he was not so eager to die as he seemed to be a moment since.

"I thought you wanted to die!" said the giant with a sneer. "Williamson, you deserve to perish like a dog—you the devil whose hate of a noble Injun is deluging the Illinois in innocent blood. But they'll catch you yet, an' then you'll experience what Jack Senior did."

The terrible doom of Senior was known throughout the length and breadth of the Illinois country.

"No, no," groaned Williamson, his knees smiting one another. "I'll cut my throat first."

"They'll never give you that chance," put in Somerville, who smiled to see the terror of the justly haunted wretch.

"We're huntin' a gal—Kate Blount," said Doc Bell, addressing the cowardly trader, "an' we'll take you with us if you promise to behave decently."

"I'll do that," was the response, "and, sirs, I'll fight like a lion, when it comes to that."

"Well, it's coming to that," said the giant, "and then—"

"Hark!" whispered the youth, clutching his companion's arm.

The quartette listened, and heard footsteps in the forest.

"The Illinois is full of fiends," whispered Blount.

"And they're coming up the creek!" groaned the haunted trader, audibly.

"Speak above a whisper again, John Williamson, an' I'll toss you into the red-skins' arms," said the giant, as he laid his hand upon the trader's shoulder.

The sounds increased, and indicated the approach of a large body of Indians. They were advancing up the opposite side of the stream, and to our friends' surprise halted almost directly opposite their covert.

The starlight enabled our friends to arrive at their number, and they concluded that they were advancing against a somewhat exposed village of the Peorias not many miles distant. Immediately after kindling a fire, which they did upon halting, the chiefs came together for counsel, and Oliver Blount and the two hunters watched them with anxiety and interest. They dared not move, for the least movement might reach their enemies' ears, and, in a moment, two hundred avengers would be upon them.

Therefore, they resolved to remain where they were until the conclusion of the council, which they knew would transpire before dawn.

Wearied with his long tramp—tired of flying, no doubt, from an imaginary foe, the haunted trader dropped into a fitful slumber, while his companions watched the council.

Suddenly they were startled by a most unearthly cry.

"Avaunt! avaunt! I didn't kill Pontiac! Hellions, away! away!"

The trio were on their feet in an instant, and beheld John Williamson with frantic gestures trying to beat back the phantoms that haunted him.

His aspect was enough to frighten the spectators; but their peril and rage drove every thing else from their minds.

The trader's tone had reached the Indian camp. The council was breaking, and swarms of painted braves were rushing to the stream with their eyes fastened upon the spot where stood the seemingly doomed scouts.

Doc Bell, the giant, realizing the danger, with a dreadful anathema, sprung upon the dreamer like a tiger.

"Curse you!" he hissed, as he clutched the haunted trader's throat, and threw him above his head as though he were as light as a child. "You'll never dream of your victim again—John Williamson—never!"

He sprung to the edge of the cliff, and at a glance saw every Indian in the water below.

"My God! He's going to kill John!" cried Oliver Blount, as he darted toward the giant.

"Spare him, Doc!"

"Never!" and with his word he hurled the body out into the air, and it fell among the savages below, with a rushing sound.

"Now!" yelled the backwoods Ajax, turning suddenly upon his companions. "For your lives, run!"

The next moment they bounded into the grayish forest, with a hundred fiends yelling at their heels!

CHAPTER V
IN THE HANDS OF FATE

The Indians, consisting of representatives from each of the avenging nations, had reached the top of the bank in less time than we could record the movement, and gained perceptibly upon the flying whites from the first.

The trio kept close together, and ever and anon glanced backward to behold their dusky foes nearing them with a rapidity which betokened swift doom.

Still the wood stretched before them, and no covert, no natural stronghold in which they might attempt a defense presented itself; and no succoring volley burst upon their ears. Had they been as fresh as their pursuers were, they might hope to elude the red hands; but the respective tramps from Fort Chartres and Cahokia had fatigued them, and, even when flying for life, they felt the terrible lack of strength.

"They're going to catch us!" said Bob Somerville, the young scout, glancing over his shoulder at the howling legion.

"If we say so—yes," said the giant. "What do you say, Blount? As for myself, I'll never throw down my rifle, an' cry quarter to that troop of man-skinners. But you have a daughter, an' as they bear you but little hatred compared to that which they bear old Doc Bell, p'r'aps you'd better give up—you an' Bob, here."

"What! I surrender to them!" cried the young scout, shooting a look of indignation at the giant at his side. "Never! I'm going to stay with you, Doc. Let us run on!"

On, still on they went, and all at once the big hunter cried:

"Tree! they're goin' to shoot."

Instantly the trio sprung to trees, and simultaneously with their action a score of rifles cracked. The leaden pellets whistled about them like hail, and, staggering from the giant oak, which his hands had barely touched, Oliver Blount dropped over the trunk of a decayed tree.

"Let 'em hev it, Bob," cried the giant. "We might as well die here as any place. They've finished Oll, the red dogs hev, nor shall one feel the pain of skinning."

As the hunter finished, he thrust his long-barreled rifle forward, and the young sub-chief who was bounding toward Blount with uplifted tomahawk, reeled with a death-yell, and fell dead, as a comrade, a few feet in his rear, met a like fate by the ball from Bob Somerville's rifle.

"Now load, boy, load for yer life!" shrieked the giant, snatching the horn from his side, and with lightning rapidity proceeding to load his trusty rifle. "Beavers! Blount's not dead. Brave fellar! he's goin' to give them a blister!"

The hunter in his rough manner had spoken truly.

The sorely-wounded trader with closed teeth and avenging eyes, had raised himself on his knees, and thrust his weapon over the log—his invulnerable bulwark. The twain behind the trees watched him as they reloaded their guns, and when they saw the old man's finger press the trigger they exposed their bodies enough to see an Ottawa brave spring into the air with a death-shriek.

"Well done, Blount!" cried Bell, as the trader looked up with a smile of satisfaction, and then sunk behind the log to reload.

The Indians knew that their foes could recharge their weapons before they could engage in a hand-to-hand conflict, and, therefore, after Blount's death-shot they sought the protection of trees until they could draw another volley from the whites.

With the agility so characteristic of the red-man, they glided from tree to tree, gradually approaching their victims and trying to get in their rear.

"We're their meat, Bob," hissed Doc Bell. "It's no use disputin' *thet* point. Ef I only had that infernal Williamson hyar! But, I finished him; that's some consolation. Ha!"

With the exclamation, the giant's rifle touched his shoulder, and a yell told that some ill-fated red-man had exposed his body to the death-scout's aim. An instant later the weapons of the other whites spoke their death-tidings, and the chorus of yells that quickly followed would have done credit to the choir of the lost in Pandemonium.

The Indians to a man shot forward; and with clubbed rifles and knives griped between their teeth, Doc Bell and his companion sprung from the trees, and faced the red horde with the look of men whose lives must be purchased at a terrible cost.

Oliver Blount seemed to forget for what he had to live, and to have imbibed the spirit of his companions; for, despite his wounds, which caused his lips to twitch with acute pain, he threw himself over the log with drawn tomahawk.

"Come on, devils!" he yelled at the savages. "Come on, I say, and greet the edge of trader Blount's hatchet!"

The Indians greeted his speech with derisive yells, and when they had almost reached the desperate men, who had braced themselves for the battle to the death, a solitary rifle cracked, and Big Fox-Fire, the giant of the Delawares and the leader of the avengers, sunk to the ground without a groan.

Awe-stricken by the mysterious shot the savages executed an abrupt halt, and their eyes, staring upon some object beyond the whites, drew the attention of the latter thither.

Near fifty yards behind them, and upon the trunk of a newly-fallen tree, stood the slayer of the gigantic Delaware; and when the eyes of the hunted whites fell upon the avenger, a cry simultaneously parted their lips:

"'Tis Kate!"

Yes, in the person of the slayer, the form of Kate Blount was easily recognizable, and with a light cry which reached her father's ears, she bounded forward.

"Back, Kate, back!" shouted Oliver Blount, waving her aloof. "You can escape the fiends!"

But she did not heed his voice, for she came on, faster than ever, and with a joyful cry, in the presence of the painted denizens of the wood, she sunk upon the bosom where she had pillowed her head so oft in happier days.

"Kate, my own Kate!" cried Oliver Blount, in a voice tremulous with a father's emotion; and then he looked through his tears to the giant as if to say: "Doc Bell, we'll live for my daughter."

The giant understood that mute appeal. He dropped his rifle to the ground, and caused the blade of his scalping-knife to quiver in the bark of the tree.

"I'm goin' to live fur the gal—fur Kate," he cried, glancing at his protege, who had followed his example. "That gal ar' too brave to die, an' suthin' might turn up."

"Yes, yes, we'll stand by Kate Blount, so long as we have life left," said Somerville, and his lustrous eyes, dimmed by the meeting of father and child, wandered to the beautiful owner of that name whom he had long in secret, and late, openly, loved.

Oliver Blount released his child after a moment's fond embrace, and his action broke the spell which had bound the rude red horde.

They started forward, not with uplifted weapons, but with empty hands, to take possession of their prisoners, for they could not mistake the meaning of the quivering knife and grounded rifle.

"Yes, we're yours," said Doc Bell, addressing the Indians, as he held forth his arms to receive the twisted sinews; "an' ye may thank yer Manitou that this gal came when she did. She's saved many a life to-day, she hez; an' we're goin' to stan' by her through thick an' thin. Come, Bob, don't pervoke the Injun; act decently, ef it ar' ag'in' the grain. 'Tain't the first time we war tied."

The young scout was about to strike a fierce young Ojibwa who had spat in his face, but the giant's words unclinched his hand, and he told the red-man that they would meet again.

The Indians made no noisy demonstration over the surrender of the whites, but their lowering looks boded ill for their captives; and Doc Bell's acute senses heard the younger warriors whispering about dull knives, and he saw them mimicking the flaying process with fiendish contortions of face and form.

But he did not communicate his observations to his fellow-prisoners; he would not horrify them with their doom.

The pale-faces were soon bound, and the victors turned their faces toward Cahokia creek again.

The trader found that the bullet in his thigh did not impede his progress, and flinging pain to the winds, he managed to keep pace with the savages.

Big Fox-Fire and the fallen braves were borne before the party, and when the spot where the council had convened the preceding night was reached, the band halted, and the giant looked around for the haunted trader.

But that personage was not visible.

"He drowned in the stream!" he muttered, to himself. "Well, he is out of the world at any rate, an' I calculate as how the world is the gainer."

Almost immediately after the halt the captives were bound to separate trees, and the savages coolly proceeded to discuss their morning meal.

"I'm as hungry as a wolf!" growled Doc Bell, throwing a wistful look upon the huge slices of venison that surmounted the sticks which the Indians held over the blaze. "I could gnaw my moccasins, an' get a good meal out ov an Injun's scalp-lock. Ha! here's comes a slice. Beavers!"

An Indian near six feet in hight, and as straight as an Assiniboin arrow, whose raven hair covered his otherwise naked shoulders, had risen from the fire, and was approaching the hunter with a huge slice of roasted venison.

Doc Bell had noticed him before he left the blaze, and he felt assured in his own mind that he had encountered that stalwart form before. But he never knew a savage of such particular build, who owned such a mass of hair. A moment later, when the Indian wheeled and displayed his features to the hunter, the exclamation which concluded his mutterings escaped his lips.

"The pale-face is as hungry as the nestlings whose mother is no more," said the Indian, pausing before the giant, whose sturdy eyes were filled with wonder and amazement.

"Hungry!" he cried, in an overtone; "I should reckon I was hungry," and then his voice dropped to a whisper. "Nehonesto, I could eat you, hair an' all."

The hunter's words threw a strange light into the Indian's eyes. He stepped forward quite impulsively, and his right hand jerked the unnecessarily broad deer-skin strap of his paint-bag from its accustomed position on his tawny breast. A second later his hand dropped to his side, but the giant had caught sight of a crescent star, again hidden by the strap.

Then, in silence, Nehonesto, as Doc Bell had styled the Indian, satisfied his hunger, and in like manner his fellow-captives were fed.

"There goes a friend!" murmured the hunter, as Nehonesto returned to the fire, without having spoken a hopeful word. "I thought the fellow dead, an' it's the Almighty's doin's thet we've come together again. Wonder where Tarpah is, an' Mohesto an' Otter Eyes, an' the rest of our brotherhood? Thank God for Nehonesto, at least. But, suppose the Injuns should take a notion to finish us to-day, what could Nehonesto do?" and away down in his heart he answered, "Nothing!"

But he kept his eyes riveted upon the Indian, who never deigned him a glance, but ate his venison in stolid silence among the congregation of chiefs.

The hunter would fain have bidden his companions hope; but he was too widely separated from them to converse in whispers, and, besides, an Indian stood between him and them. A word might seal his doom.

For two long hours the chiefs were holding low converse, and the giant hunter saw Nehonesto among them.

What would the Indians do?

All at once a wild yell came from the cliff on the opposite side of the deep creek.

Every eye turned to the elevated spot, and upon the very edge of the declivity stood a red Amazon, whose aspect was most terrible.

"Who guided that she-devil hither?" cried Doc Bell. "I know her an' she knows me, an' to-day I'd sooner meet a thousand mad wolves than Coleola, the Snake Queen of the Delawares. Thar'll be suthin' dreadful to pay now. Nehonesto, where are you?"

CHAPTER VI
COLEOLA AND NEHONESTO

After slaying the Indian who had pursued her from the hunted Peoria's cave home, Kate Blount continued her flight unmolested. She ran forward quite rapidly until her limbs grew weary, and her gait dwindled down to a fast walk. She had noted the ground over which she had passed a few brief hours before with Swamp Oak, and now knew that she was hurrying toward Cahokia creek.

Suddenly a chorus of wild yells burst upon her ears, and with a throbbing heart she ensconced herself in the top of a fallen tree, from whence she witnessed the conflict between the war-party, her father and friends.

She saw that the Indians did not seek the lives of the trio, and the countenances of the whites told her that they were going to fight to the death—that they, seeing their cause hopeless, would force the red-skins to slay them for self-preservation.

And well, too, she knew that her presence would change the tide of affairs, and to preserve the life of her father—preserve it, perhaps, for a fate worse than death by the tomahawk, she slew Big Fox-Fire, and became the avengers' prisoner.

When the yell which announced Coleola's appearance on the cliffs opposite the war-party, and Kate beheld the mad Snake Queen, a pallor flitted over her cheeks, and she glanced at her father, who was bound to a sapling scarce five feet away.

"An unpitying demoness has arrived upon the scene," he said, returning her fearful look with one full of sadness. "Coleola can rule the passions of this band of red-skins, as supremely as the master the actions of his slave. Girl, expect no mercy at her hands; the bare sight of her has dissipated all my hopes of escape."

While he spoke, the Snake Queen and her followers descended, and crossed the creek by wading.

Coleola's dark orbs flashed fire when they fell upon her late captive, and scarcely had she emerged from the water, when with a panther-like yell she darted forward and halted before the fair white girl.

Her passion kept the Indians aloof, and with distended eyes they watched her wild, mad movements.

"The she white serpent crept from the hole in the ground and slew Segagi!" she hissed, and with a dextrous movement she uncoiled the serpents that encircled her neck, and thrust them forward until their forked tongues almost touched Kate's face. "Yes," she hissed, more fiendishly than ever, "in the great forest, a prey to the wolf and panther, lies Segagi, Coleola's most trusted spy. And does the White Snake hope to boast of her shot, behind the walls of the great fort?"

She paused, expecting a reply, but the brave girl rewarded her with none, and striking her cheeks with the whip-like tails of the snakes she drew back a pace.

"The pale girl must talk to the Manitou!" she continued, "for Coleola's snakes shall writhe in her bosom when the fair skin has been torn away."

A shudder swept to the hearts of the captives at this terrible announcement. The face of Oliver Blount grew white as snow when he looked upon his daughter, and thought of the fate that the furious Snake Queen had marked out for her.

The leaders of the war-party did not attempt to interfere with the Delaware demoness; they feared her as they feared the evil spirits; and there were many who believed that she was the natural daughter of Watchemenetoc, for no one, not even the white-haired chiefs, could tell how and when she first appeared to the Delaware tribe.

From Kale Blount her eyes swept to the form of the wood Hercules, and a terrific yell pealed from her throat as she sprung before Doc Bell, and glared upon him with the ferocity of the whelp-robbed jungle tigress.

"Wal," said the hunter, calmly, "I hup I see you. It's been a long time since we've met. I b'lieve I war a prisoner in yer town then, and it fut'hermore occurs to me that I left that old sorcerer, Conestoga, whom you called yer husband, as dead as Indians ginerally become. Ye couldn't keep Doc Bell in the ring, eh, Coleola!"

The Snake Queen remained unmoved until the hunter uttered the name of his victim. Then a cry of rage parted her lips and she stepped nearer, her eyes spitting their anger into Bell's face. But, the old hunter finished his sentence undaunted, and returned her insane glare with a look of calmness.

He had raised her anger to the highest pitch attainable, and when he saw her long knife flash from beneath the tunic which habited her giant frame, he gave himself up for lost, and smiled upon the deadly blade.

With a muttered anathema the Snake Queen threw the steel aloft, seeing nothing but the slayer of her lord, forgetting, in her eagerness to drink his blood, the tortures she could inflict upon him; and contrary to her vengeful resolves, decreeing to him a comparatively painless death.

The rattlesnakes writhed around the tawny arm thrown aloft, and seemed intent upon reaching the blade held far above her head—the blade that trembled on the scent of death. For a second the mad-woman glared at the hunter without striking, and then she stepped back to deliver the blow with a tiger-like spring.

The Indians saw this, and held their breath. The other captives could not avert their eyes from the doom of the giant, their companion in misfortune.

"White dog, die!" shrieked Coleola, and like the panther darted upon her victim.

But the knife never reached the hunter's heart; an arm as red as that of the would-be murderess' interposed, and when she gazed upon the intruder, she beheld him planted as firmly as the oak between her and the hunter!

It was Nehonesto!

"The Snake Queen must reach the big man's heart through Nehonesto's," he said, calmly returning the flash of the baffled woman's eyes.

"He is Nehonesto's brother, and Nehonesto will die for him. Now let Coleola strike! now let her throw her snakes upon the Ojibwa."

A cry of rage welled from the Snake Queen's throat, and she retreated several feet, tearing the snakes from her arm as she executed the movement. Her eyes were fixed upon Nehonesto; she saw no other form than his, and as she paused, with the rapidity of a flash of lighting one of the rattlers went hissing through the air!

The Ojibwa saw it, but did not move. He merely threw his knife arm before his face, and flung the serpent aside with a dexterity that drew a shout of applause from the red spectators. He flung the snake away with all his strength, and with a shriek of horror he saw it wrap itself around the throat of the trader's daughter!

A shout of triumph cleft the air;—it came from Coleola's throat; and the second snake had left her arm when Nehonesto darted toward our heroine!

He griped the immense serpent—immense for a rattlesnake—with his bare hands, and tore it from its dreadful embrace, with such fury that it snapped in twain, leaving the tail dangling from his hand, while the hideous head clung by the fangs to Kate Blount's cheek!

At the sight of the maiden's peril a cry of horror burst from the throats of the Indians, and even Coleola forsook her station, and, with many others, sprung forward.

The white girl's head had dropped upon her bosom, and the pallor of death shrouded her face. Instantly Nehonesto's knife severed her bonds, and when the red-men crowded around the spot, he had lowered her to the ground, and was holding the mouth of his leathern flask to her colorless lips.

Pity instantly took the place of vengeance, and upon every face, save that of Coleola's, that sweet angel sat enthroned.

Kate Blount was conscious, and she drank deeply of the contents of the Ojibwa's flask. She knew that whisky counteracted the effects of the poison of the rattlesnake in the human system, and she felt its effects ere the flask was drained.

"The Lone Dove of the pale-faces will not tread the dark wood," said Nehonesto, noting with a smile the effect of the fire-water. "She will live—live to become Nehonesto's captive."

"No! no!" cried Coleola, at this, "the White Snake lives to die—to be skinned alive by the blunt knife of Coleola. She caught her in the Swamp Oak's cave, but she fled like the hunted fox, while Coleola sought the red dog that stole her child many moons ago. But ah! Coleola caught her child, and from her mouth she has plucked her lying tongue."

As she finished, Nehonesto rose to his feet, and faced the chief—the leader of the war-band.

"Chiefs, decide between Nehonesto and Coleola," he said. "He claims the pale flower, and the giant hunter. Shall they die by the knife of a mad-woman—they and their brethren," and he glanced at the trader and Somerville—"or shall they become the captives of Nehonesto, the War Eagle of the Ojibwas?"

A fateful silence followed the Indian's speech, and the chiefs addressed looked into each other's faces.

"Decide for Coleola!" cried the Snake Queen, "or the plagues of Watchemenetoc shall fall upon the red-men like rain-drops, and of all this band not one shall sleep in the lodges again."

The cheeks of the sachems paled at this, and trembling at the dreadful threat, the warriors shrunk from the demoness, shouting:

"Give the pale-faces to Coleola, and let her skin them, else we fall like blades of grass in the country of the Peorias."

The chiefs were dismayed, and the captives and Nehonesto read in their terror-stricken faces the decision. Suddenly Odatha stepped forward to announce the decision, but before his lips parted, a shrill cry burst upon the ears of all, and, turning, they discovered a solitary Indian running toward them, along the Cahokia's bank.

He wore the habiliments of a Piankishaw warrior, and paused all breathless in the circle of red-men that surrounded the white captives.

Then he was recognized.

"Why comes the Little Coon alone to the war eagles of the Illinois?" demanded Odatha.

"He comes from the Yellow Bloodhound," answered the new arrival, glancing around upon the prisoners with mingled surprise and triumph. "He ran before his people who are coming up the deep creek in canoes. They seek what Odatha has found," and again his eyes fell upon the captives.

Odatha understood the sentence.

"Yes, Odatha has found the pale-faces," said that worthy. "Why trails the Yellow Bloodhound them?"

"They slew Segowatha."

The Ottawa caught the runner's arm and shot him a look of blank astonishment, while the other chiefs and warriors contracted the circle with exclamations of disbelief and wonder.

"Yes, the pale-faced girl or the Peoria dog, Swamp Oak, slew Segowatha. The Yellow Bloodhound fell beneath the dog's knife, but he leads his band upon the trail again. They have sworn by the Manitou to tear the pale-faces' hearts from them; and let the arm raised to tear the white snakes away drop before they come. Like a whirlwind, they can not be stopped."

He paused, and, glancing at Nehonesto and Coleola Odatha spoke.

"We must not thwart the Yellow Bloodhound," he said. "He is a mighty whirlwind, and when he comes the pale-faces must become his—that he may avenge, according to his oath, the death of Segowatha. Coleola—"

He reverted his eyes to the mad red-woman, but with her remaining snake she was forcing a path through the throng of braves, and her warriors were following in her wake.

She heard herself addressed, but she did not pause, and when Odatha sprung forward to arrest her progress that he might tell her what he wished, one of her braves pushed him back, and, transfixed with irresolution, he beheld her swim the creek and climb the cliffs on the opposite bank.

"When the Yellow Bloodhound comes, Coleola tarries not," she cried, looking down upon the war band; "but had Odatha given the pale-faced girl and the big hunter to her, she would have stayed and faced the dog whose throat she longs to cut. Between Coleola and the Yellow Bloodhound flows the river of darkness, and some day or some night she meets him on the bank, and then the yelp of the dog will be heard for the last time. Coleola goes, but she will come again, and the plagues of the Manitou shall fall upon Odatha and his red snakes. The whites shall yet be Coleola's; they shall not be skinned by the Yellow Bloodhound. Whoever slays one of Coleola's braves shall fall before her, and the she White Snake shot Segagi! Odatha, forget nothing that has fallen from Coleola's lips. Snakes, into the dark woods. Away!"

As she uttered the last word, she shook her snake at the mute spectators, and, whirling on her heel, sprung from sight.

"Then the pale-faces are the Yellow Bloodhound's?" said Nehonesto, addressing Odatha.

"Odatha has spoken," was the reply, and Nehonesto, with a determined expression, turned to Kate again.

She had almost entirely recovered from the serpent bite, and under Nehonesto's protection was permitted to pillow her head upon her father's breast.

"Kate, Kate, thank God you yet live, despite the machinations of our enemies," said the old man, bowing his head to receive his daughter's kiss. "I know now that He watches over us."

"Yes, father, but whose arm will interpose between us and the knife of the Yellow Bloodhound?" asked Kate.

Despite his hopings, Oliver Blount groaned.

"Oh, Heavenly Father, why does such a fiend as Jules Bardue curse the earth? Oh, that Swamp Oak's knife had reached his heart."

If curses could kill, the Yellow Bloodhound, as the creole was styled by his adopted tribe, would have fallen dead long before the opening of our story, for the old trader had cursed him as man had never before cursed his fellow.

As the moments passed, the Indians grew impatient for the arrival of Segowatha's Avengers. The captives had been taken from the trees that they might not afford marks for Coleola's rifles, for the savages feared that the Snake Queen would steal back, and satiate her vengeance by dispatching the whites from the cliffs.

"All together once more," said Doc Bell, despite the savage looks of their guards, "an' I'm gettin' anxious myself to see that ar' Bloodhound."

"We die when he comes!" said Somerville; "but we'll die like men."

"That's talkin', boy; but we ain't dead yit," said the giant, with a faint smile. "We didn't die when Coleola came, and I'd sooner meet the Yellow Bloodhound than she—yes, by a long shot. We've got one true friend in this pack of devils, an' ye've seen a sample ov his nerve. Nehonesto is the only member ov the moon-scar band that I've see'd fur four years, and I war thinkin' erbout others awhile ago. Five ov us—four Injuns an' me—formed that band on the Saginaw six years ago—afore I see'd you, boy—an' a part ov our oath was to die if need be for one another. An' I tell you Nehonesto is jest ready to die for us. Look how that cursed Little Coon watches him; the little Ojibwa suspects his giant brother, which is bad fur us. I'd like to know where we'll be to-morrow."

"In eternity, perhaps," said Oliver Blount, who had listened attentively to the giant's words.

"Mebbe so," said Bell; "but I've never been thar yet. I don't care fur my old self. My anxiety is fur your gal—your Kate, Oll."

"And my Kate, too," murmured Bob Somerville, inaudibly.

"Fear not for me," cried the trader's daughter. "I want my fate to be yours. I can die like a woman."

"But the Bloodhound won't kill you, Kate," said the giant. "He reserves you for a fate worse than death."

A fearful determination overspread Kate Blount's face, and, through clenched teeth, she hissed:

"Never!"

CHAPTER VII
THE AVENGERS BAFFLED

Night in the forest of the Illinois.

Not a star is missing in the azure canopy, and the notes of the nightingale tinkle musically in the freshening breeze.

The cry of the panther is not heard; the owl seems to be feasting himself upon some delicious morsel won by his prying eyes and sharp claws, for his hoot reëchoes not through the star-lit wood, nor does the frightful howl of the wolf, the terror of new countries, disturb the slumbers of nature.

But through the forests stalk the enemies of mankind, proving that "man is a human wolf." The wily red-skin is abroad, either as Pontiac's avenger, reddening his hatchet with the blood of his fellow-creature, or as the hunted Peoria, Kaskaskia or Cahokia, flying from the demons unchained by a barrel of English rum.

Not far from the scenes of our romance the war of extirpation had raged with terrible fury. Those English families that failed to shelter themselves in Cahokia or Fort Chartres had either been butchered by the crimson devils or were fugitives with no spot whereon to lay their heads safe from the tomahawk of the avengers.

Upon the night described above an Indian was pushing his way through the forest, and following the course of the famous Cahokia Creek, not far from its boundaries. His step proclaimed him young, and well versed in the tortuous ways of the wood, for in the dim light he avoided the dry twig or the decaying log that cracks beneath the foot, and leaped the treacherous root with the precision of one traveling in the broad light of day.

He was following no trail; on the contrary, he seemed careless regarding his whereabouts, but hurried on as though some unseen hand was leading him to a certain destination.

He reached a point at length where a rivulet debouches into the Cahokia, and there, for the first time in several hours, he halted.

"They are not far from the Peoria now," he murmured, looking to the priming of the long barreled rifle he had trailed at his side. "Swamp Oak knows that the Yellow Bloodhound dares not carry the Lone Dove to the big bands of Pontiac's mad dogs, for they would tear her to pieces, even as the wolf rends the lamb, for she slew Segowatha. All his big talks would not save the Lone Dove; the red-men of the north loved Segowatha too well. But—hist!"

The Peoria crouched at his self warning, and slunk into the shadow of a tree.

A footstep had fallen upon his ears, and presently a giant form appeared against the whitened side of a deadened oak. It was the form of a man, and a close look told the Indian that the person was the very one for whose whereabouts he was searching.

"Ha!" he muttered, "the Yellow Bloodhound is abroad—he has left his band, and stolen deeper in the forest for what? The wolf never roams the woods for nothing; the fox leaves his den to prey."

For a minute the creole (for indeed the giant form belonged to Jules Bardue) exhibited himself to the lone watcher, and then disappeared as suddenly as he had come upon the stage.

He plunged into the mouth of the tributary above-mentioned, and waded to the opposite shore, followed, with the cunning of the wolf, by the Peoria youth, who never took his eyes from the form just visible in the dim starlight.

The Yellow Bloodhound did not dream of the snake-like form that crept on his trail, and when he disappeared over the brow of a thickly-wooded acclivity, a short distance from the Cahokia, an exclamation of satisfaction parted the Peoria's lips, and, rising to his feet, he bounded forward.

The sight that greeted his vision when he gained the summit of the hill, elicited no manifestations of surprise, and, calmly leaning against a tree, he viewed the scenes that lay at his feet.

A fire was dying at the foot of the declivity, and its flickering light weirdly clothed a lot of recumbent Indians. They lay in all positions, unconscious of the proximity of a deadly foe, and Swamp Oak griped his tomahawk vengefully as he thought of their late deeds of revenge.

He saw the creole step over a sleeping chief, and speak a few words to a guard who leaned against a tree, with eyes fixed upon three white men lying bound upon the ground not far away.

"Watchemenetoc is abroad to-night," muttered the Peoria, as his eyes swept the camp for a particular object. "Where is the Lone Dove? The

Yellow Bloodhound bore her from Odatha's war-braves, but she is not with him now. Has she taken her wing and left the lair of the wolf? No, no; she would not desert her parent."

A puzzled expression appeared upon the Indian's face. Kate Blount was not in the creole's camp. Swamp Oak had witnessed the Bloodhound's separation, late the preceding day, from the war-party, and with the three male prisoners he had taken the trader's daughter. He declared that he intended to convey them to the large body of red avengers who were devastating the country round about Cahokia, and there, over the putrid corpse of Segowatha, flay them alive. The creole tried to induce Odatha to accompany him; but the chief refused, and again resumed his march for the doomed Peoria village.

Swamp Oak, whose thrilling adventures, since Coleola's bloodthirsty murder in his cave-home, shall presently fall from his own lips, did not at once, after the separation of Segowatha's Avengers and the war-party, throw himself upon the trail of the former; but had followed the latter for reasons best known to himself.

If he had followed the Yellow Bloodhound, he might have witnessed our heroine's mysterious disappearance from the band, while now regarding her fate he was left in the dark.

The white captives were wide awake.

From the summit of the hill Swamp Oak could see the glitter of their eyes, as they regarded the Bloodhound and their guard conversing in low tones.

The remainder of the avenging band—twenty in number—were sound asleep, and presently the creole glided from the guard and dropped near the dying fire.

The Peoria was conscious now of the working of some deep plot: he read it in the renegade's appearance in the woods; his conference with the guards, and his return to his blanketed couch, from whence he saw him casting sly glances at the sentinel.

Presently a wild cry pealed from the guard's throat, and every Indian, roused from slumber, sprung instantly to their feet with drawn weapons! They rushed to the dusky sentinel, loudly demanding the cause of the startling cry; and he, appearing half-frightened to death slunk behind the Yellow Bloodhound, and pointed to the spot occupied by the captives.

One glance at the trio drew a wild yell from the Avengers, for they saw that Kate Blount was missing!

"Where is the she White Snake?" demanded the creole, fiercely, and he clutched the red guard's throat, as though he would choke the life from his body.

"The wolf stole her while Ipigena leaned against the tree, and with closed eyes saw himself a boy again," stammered the Indian.

Still clutching the Indian's throat, the creole turned to the maddened crowd:

"The red dog has slept!" he said, "but we must not blame him. We have walked many miles through the forest, striking here and there the enemies of our race, and Ipigena must sleep, for he is weary. But, braves, the White Adder that stung Segowatha must not escape. Search the wood, for she is not far away. My eyes opened when the moon hung on yonder limb, and she was beside her father. Go, Avengers—Pontiac's mad dogs—to the trail!"

An instant later the creole and Ipigena were alone.

"What does this mean?" asked Blount of his companions.

"It means simply that the most infernal deviltry is afoot," answered the giant hunter. "I see through every bit of it now. That Injun who came an' took Kate into the wood was nobody else but the Bloodhound, an' that guard played sleepy to deceive us."

"But why did he take Kate away from the midst of the band he rules?"

"He rules this lot of red cut-throats, but he don't rule the band around Cahokia—not by a terrible sight. Why, Oll Blount, they'd tear yer gal to pieces on sight, an' ther Yaller Bloodhound knows this. Tharfore, he's hid her away with the knowledge ov half o' the red skunks with him now. Thar be some here to whom he daren't tell his plans. Segowatha's sons is with him."

"Will they not find Kate?"

The father's words were closed in a fearful tone.

"No; Bardue ain't the man to stow her away under a brush heap, an' then turn twenty Injuns on her trail," answered the giant; "my word for it, they won't find yer gal, Oll. It 'pears to me thet thar's caves around here."

"Oh, God," groaned the anxious parent, "now that my dear child is in the sole power of a fiend, protect her."

"He'll do it, Oll; he'll do it," said Doc Bell. "He's helped me out o' many a scrape; but the Injuns ar' comin' back, madder nor thunder. I told yer they wouldn't find the gal."

Sure enough the savages, with disappointed visages, and fierce scowls upon the captives, were returning from a fruitless search, and with wild yells that made the woods ring, they gathered around the Yellow Bloodhound, clamoring for a pale-face's blood.

"Blood! blood!" yelled the son of Segowatha, a young and fierce-looking warrior; "my father's spirit calls for the red tide of the white girl's heart; but now that she has gone—now that Watchemenetoc has borne her away—the spirit that stands before Little Wolf points to the three pale men, saying, 'Skin them! skin them and drink their blood to me in the hollow of your hands.'"

His words threw a majority of the band into a frenzy impossible to describe. They yelled "Blood! blood!" like demons, and danced about the captives before the Yellow Bloodhound could find his tongue.

"We have sworn to bring the pale-faces to the uncovered grave of Segowatha, there to tear out their hearts and drink their blood," he said. "Shall that oath be broken?"

"Yes, yes," shrieked the blood-mad avengers. "The Yellow Bloodhound must close his mouth against us. The prisoners must die."

"Then let them die!" hissed Jules Bardue, and in a lower tone he added to the guard: "They might escape between here and the big band. But they'll never find the girl, never!"

With bloodthirsty eagerness the savages, Ojibwas, Ottawas, Pottawatomies and Miamis, headed by Little Wolf, made preparations for the torture. A party brought a quantity of stones from the creek, and upon them the devils proceeded to blunt their knives, that the captives' skin might be torn from their bodies with the most excruciating torture.

The giant looked calmly upon the devilish preliminaries, and a shudder stole to young Somerville's heart. A sad expression wreathed the trader's features, telling that he thought not of himself, but of his daughter.

"We're in for it now, I guess," muttered the hunter. "What! Bob, first? No! no! spare the boy; take me first. I've killed the most ov yer dog-devils. I've scalped full twenty ov yer chiefs!"

But the flayers paid no attention to the old hunter; they cut young Somerville's bonds, and proceeded to strip his clothes from his body.

"What a pretty skin!" exclaimed a young brave, striking the scout's breast with his knife. "Ha! the red blood comes; it flows like Segowatha's flowed."

He sunk the point of his knife beneath our hero's skin, but no cry of pain followed the brutal action; and suddenly, stripped to the waist, the youth found himself jerked to his feet.

Two young braves held him, and amid the flourish of knives and shouts of vengeance, they turned to the death-tree.

"Shall I die without an effort for life?" muttered Somerville; "die when I might live to snatch Kate from the Bloodhound's jaws? Never!"

As his lips grated the last word through clinched teeth, he hurled the two braves aside, and suddenly wheeling, dashed through the circle of knives, and soon disappeared in the somber recesses of the forest!

His action disturbed the would-be flayers; but they quickly dashed away in swift pursuit.

"You can't catch Bob Somerville!" cried the giant hunter. "He's the best runner in the Illinois, an' with the thought ov bein' skinned alive to grease his' joints, he'll be worse nor a streak o' lightnin'."

It was as the hunter had predicted. The scout's pursuers soon returned empty-handed, and turned their fury upon him. The Yellow Bloodhound, incensed at the young man's escape, now aided them; hitherto, for show, he had stood aloof.

A dozen fiends carried the giant to the tree, and the sinewy rope was passed around his neck.

But, as the son of Segowatha attempted to knot the cord, a rifle-shot rose above the vengeful yells, and, dropping the sinews, the young chief staggered from the tree with a dark spot between his little eyes.

With ghastly features the braves shrunk from the fatal flaying post, and the cowardly creole threw himself behind a tree.

A half-smothered cry burst from Doc Bell's heart, and, as Little Wolf struck the ground, he darted from the stake. The affrighted red-skins drew back before him, and from the trembling hands of one he snatched a knife, burying it in the owner's breast, with a backward thrust!

A single bound brought him to the spot where Oliver Blount lay.

He stooped over the trader, and when he rose erect again, a moment later, Oliver was at his side.

They bounded forward together, as a deafening peal of thunder broke over their heads! They looked up, and saw above a canopy of inky darkness!

"The Almighty's with us!" exclaimed Blount, as they dashed away.

"They won't foller now, Oll," said Doc Bell; "but they'll hunt us to the death yit. Wonder where Bob is?"

"And my child!" groaned the father, and a moment later he asked: "Where are we going?"

"To a hidin'-place, in course," answered the giant, and clutching the trader's hand he abruptly turned aside.

CHAPTER VIII
THE BLOODHOUND'S HOWL

"I wonder where Blount and Doc are. But, why do I wonder? I left them ready for that torture, the bare thought of which causes my flesh to creep, and no doubt I am the only one left. The only one? No, there's Kate, and my life-duty is now to find her—to track the Bloodhound to his kennel, and snatch her from the fate he has in store for her—a fate worse than death."

The speaker, as the reader has already surmised, was the young scout— Robert Somerville—nicknamed Bob, by his giant tutor and companion, now, as he thought, dead.

The youth ran several miles before he paused, almost ready to sink to the earth with utter exhaustion, and when he found that the red-skins had given over the pursuit, he crept under the projecting banks of a ravine, and fell into a sound slumber. When he awoke to the dangerous realities that surrounded him, the sun was peering down upon him, and the birds were singing among the bushes that hid his retreat. But, he did not stir; he did not seek the food his stomach craved, for well he knew what number of red marauders swarmed through the forests, and he believed that, as soon as practicable, Segowatha's avengers would throw themselves upon his trail, determined to hunt him to the doors of doom.

During the day, therefore, he kept his retreat. Parting the bushes he watched the leaden clouds sweep across the sky, and tried to forget the fate of his friends in the twitter of the love-making orioles and the calls of the finches. And when at last the sun sunk below the ravine, and the shadows deepened, he crept, like the hunted wolf, from his covert, and reconnoitered the hollow before ascending to the wood above, when he spoke, as the reader has heard, regarding his friends.

Bob Somerville was not a novice in the ways of the wood. Under the eye of Doc Bell he had mastered the hunter and trapper's profession, and he had faced the savage on the banks of the Miami a year prior to the opening of our story. The twain encountered the red-men with the bravery so characteristic of the spirits of the new-found West, until a whole tribe rose against them, and hunted them from the fertile lands of Ohio. Then they came to the country of the Illinois, and accidentally, one day our hero met the trader's daughter, to whom in love he became inseparably connected.

All unarmed he stood alone in the great woods, and longed, actually sighed for the trusty rifle which no doubt rested upon some tawny shoulder, or lay broken at the foot of a tree.

"I must be about four miles from the mouth of Mink Creek," he continued, after a pause, during which he had heard no sounds save the long howl of the wolf, a mile away. "Kate is hidden near there, and in her hour of danger I must be near. Yes, I will save her, though I be flayed alive in the performance of my duty."

The thought of the fair girl's situation impelled the young hunter from the spot, and a moment later he was hurrying toward the scene of the preceding chapter, and, perhaps, into the jaws of death.

Almost immediately after his escape, a thunder-storm broke over the forests, and the leaves, still saturated with water, now gave forth no sound. Bob Somerville was rejoiced at this. The prowling savage could not hear his tread, and he blessed the rain as he had never blessed it before.

After an hour's labor he found himself upon the scene of his escape, the night previous.

He listened upon the hill a long time before he descended, and then it was with wildly-throbbing heart. He expected to find the mangled bodies or charred bones of the giant and the trader, but in this he was agreeably disappointed. He found nothing to indicate that they were dead; but he found their rifles with his own, battered out of shape against a tree.

Not a foe was in sight. The silence that brooded over him was the silence of death, and for many minutes he leaned against a tree and planned deeply for the future.

"They have not returned to Cahokia," he muttered, referring to the avengers. "They will not leave this country without me, nor will the Bloodhound desert Kate until the gust of war has left the land. Now, where shall I go—what do? Here I am as weaponless as the blind worm. Oh—"

A plash in the water scarcely twenty feet from him broke the chain of his murmurings, and he crouched at the foot of the tree like the panther ready for a spring. His forest experience told him that the noise had been caused by a human foot, and presently his keen eye detected a statue-like object on the bank of the Cahokia.

That it was the figure of a white man, our hero well knew, for the head between him and the stars that peeped through a rift in the foliage was crowned with a fur cap, and not by the plumes or scalp-lock of the Indian. The young scout held his breath while he regarded the man, trying in vain to fix his identity, and when, all at once, he heard the mysterious one communing with himself, he bent forward with an eagerness which almost proved his doom.

For his foot, which he moved to secure an easier position, snapped a tiny twig and caused the stranger with hastily-drawn knife to step directly toward him.

But still ten feet distant he paused, and after listening a moment, sent the hoot of the little horned-owl from his throat.

Bob Somerville almost started forward at this signal, for he had often heard it from the lips of Doc Bell, and now he believed that the Hercules before him was his old and tried friend. But, notwithstanding this belief, he resolved to be cautious, and answered the signal with the notes of the nightingale.

At this the giant stepped forward, paused within gun's-length of the scout, and whispered:

"Nogawa!"

A strange thrill darted to young Somerville's heart.

The voice had betrayed the speaker—had declared him the Yellow Bloodhound!

For a moment the young scout did not move; but he was concentrating his strength for a spring.

He answered the creole's whisper with an Ojibwa "here," and, as the villain moved forward, he shot upward and struck him with all the strength he could summon.

So sudden and unexpected was the assault, that the knife dropped from Jules Bardue's hand, and when he struck the earth he found the scout upon his breast, and saw his own glittering blade in dangerous proximity to his craven heart.

"I've got the upper hand now, Jules Bardue!" hissed Somerville, glaring upon his enemy with the ferocity of the tiger; "and no doubt there'll be a dead Frenchman hereabouts when I stand erect again. Now, sir devil, answer what questions I choose to put."

The creole did not reply; but smiled sardonically in his foeman's eyes.

"In the first place, where is the girl—Kate Blount?"

No answer.

The question was repeated, and the knife flew aloft—drawn upward by deadly intent.

"Ha! ha! ha!" laughed the Yellow Bloodhound, with forced gayety. "How sweet it is to die revenged! The girl is hidden forever from your eyes—she never meets her father again. She refused to become Madame Bardue once, and old Blount slashed my back till it bled like a deer's throat. Now I'm almost even with him; but I'd like to get the old hound into my clutches again."

"He is out of them now?"

"Yes, curse him!"

"Thank God!" ejaculated Somerville. "But I will not talk with you. You'd talk here till morning. Where is the girl?"

The creole laughed devilishly with his steel-gray eyes, and the scout gritted his teeth with rage and disappointment.

"Then here ends your accursed villainies!" he cried. "If Kate is dead, I'll avenge her; if living I'll find her without you to baffle me."

The lips closed with determined emphasis over the last word, and a second later the shining steel descended.

It entered the broad breast of the Yellow Bloodhound, and with a shriek, scarce half-human, he sprung upward, hurling our hero from him as if he were a child. Upon his feet, the fiend reeled a moment as though he would fall, and then, seemingly having gained control of himself, he wheeled and darted toward the creek from which he had lately emerged.

It was the pain shot throughout his body by the penetrating steel that drove him to his feet, and soon, no doubt, he would fall, like the death-wounded stag, when the gush of strength had spent its force.

The scout noted the effect of his blow with a cry of horror, and darted after the wounded creole, determined to put an end to the life he had but partially stricken.

The Yellow Bloodhound gained the deep creek a yard or two in advance of his pursuer, and plunged in. He sunk immediately, for his strength seemed to have deserted him; but a minute later he rose to the surface of the blood-tinged water, a short distance below the spot where Bob Somerville stood.

"Ha! there he is!" cried the young man, and he darted down-stream, with his eyes fastened upon his foe.

A minute later the avenging knife might have found the heart it had missed a moment before, had not a dark object sprung from the rushes, almost beneath the scout's very feet, and a red hand griped his arm.

Young Somerville turned upon the intruder with a low cry, and threw the gory blade aloft to descend upon a search for another heart, when a strange laugh greeted his ears, and he heard his forest appellation—Young Hunter—spoken in a tone which he had heard before.

Instantly the knife dropped to his side, and he found himself face to face with Nehonesto!

CHAPTER IX
THE FOES AT BAY

"Hist, Young Hunter!"

These words dropped in cautious tones from Nehonesto's lips a moment after his recognition by the young scout.

Bob Somerville listened, and heard the panther-like tread of an Indian. Suddenly the Ojibwa touched his shoulder, and together they crouched to the ground.

"'Tis Nogawa," whispered the scout.

"Nogawa?" returned Nehonesto, interrogatively. "Nehonesto has seen him among the lodges of the Ojibwas. Why comes he here?"

"He belongs to the Bloodhound's party," said Somerville, and then, in a few words, he told the giant savage how the creole sought for Nogawa when he (the scout) sprung upon him.

"Ha! Nogawa knows where the Lone Dove is," murmured Nehonesto, in tones of unconcealed delight. "He has been spying for his master, and—"

A bird-signal broke the sepulchral stillness of the night.

It was now patent to the twain that Jules Bardue and Nogawa had promised to meet near the mouth of Mink Creek, and that the Indian had been tardy in keeping his appointment.

Nehonesto smiled, and from his throat came the croaking of the great emerald frog.

Immediately the footsteps which had ceased, were heard nearer than before, and presently they saw the lithe form of Nogawa approaching.

Suddenly he halted, signaled, and heard the frog croak again.

Then the two friends heard him exclaim, "Yellow Chief!" and with his eyes bent upon the spot where they crouched he walked boldly and unsuspectingly into the snare!

Nehonesto sprung forward, and Nogawa found himself a prisoner!

"Who holds the eagle's pinions?" he demanded, trying to tear away from the grip of his own countryman.

"Who? Nehonesto! Nogawa came to meet the Yellow Bloodhound, and if he would find him, he must dive beneath the water and hunt among the fishes. Yes, the Yellow Bloodhound has stepped upon the trail of death; he scents blood no more in the woods of the Illinois. Nogawa knows where he hid the Lone Dove, and to the den he must lead Nehonesto and the Young Hunter."

The last words were couched in a determined tone, but the captive did not reply, he looked into Nehonesto's eyes, as though he but half-credited the words regarding the fate of his master.

"Nogawa," and as Nehonesto spoke, he drew his scalping-knife from his wampum girdle, "you must lead us to the Lone Dove. Nehonesto, like yourself, is an Ojibwa, but unless you do as he bids, the door of the lodge in the dark land will open to receive an Indian's spirit. Speak, Nogawa—what will you do?"

For a moment the young Indian's head dropped upon his breast, and when he raised it, his captors read the decision he had made in his dark eyes.

"Nogawa will obey his brother"—glancing at the knife; "what else should he do?"

"Then, quick upon the trail!" cried Somerville, who thought of the brave girl whose life, at that moment, might be in imminent danger.

The young Ojibwa obeyed by moving forward, his arm still encircled by the long fingers of Nehonesto.

"Where did the Yellow Bloodhound send Nogawa?" asked Nehonesto, as they walked cautiously down the bank of the Cahokia.

"He sent him with a band who hunted for the three pale-faces," replied the Indian, "and Nogawa was to return and tell him if his eyes had fallen upon the dire Snake Queen."

"And did Nogawa see Coleola?" asked our hero, a shudder creeping to his heart, as the dread woman appeared to his imagination, clothed in the hideousness of vengeance.

"He did!"

"And where was she?"

"She was on the bank of the creek, where the muskrats dwell."

Somerville looked at Nehonesto.

"The red hag is going to work us trouble," he said. "She will not leave this country without the scalps of all whom she hates. She hunts the Bloodhound now."

"And she hates Nehonesto as the Indian hates the copperhead," grated the Ojibwa between his set teeth.

"She may even now be near!"

"Nehonesto saw her not when he approached," replied the long-haired chief, "and Nehonesto's eyes are as sharp as the eagle's."

Thus, with dark forebodings to keep him continually alive to their presence, Bob Somerville walked on, venturing no more to question Nogawa, who seemed to be reconciled to his fate.

At length they reached the beginning of the high banks, but instead of ascending, Nogawa stepped into the water and waded on up the stream, carefully noting every thing around him. At the water's edge a thick growth of willows thrived, and bending, kissed the ripples in the center of the stream. Their well-leaved branches prevented the sharpest eye from beholding the stalks, and when the forced guide paused before the king of the weepers, Nehonesto griped his arm more tightly, and in a whisper bade him proceed.

"The Bloodhound's cave is here," replied Nogawa, and he looked up to see that no heads were peering over the cliff.

"Here!" said Nehonesto, exhibiting some astonishment, and parting the bushes, he could discover nothing that indicated the presence of a hidden home.

The young Ojibwa did not reply, but stepped forward, and a moment later the trio had vanished.

They found themselves in a gloomy passage, whose walls and ceiling they could touch with head and hands.

Nogawa led the way, unfettered now by his clansman's hand, and Bob Somerville brought up the rear, with cocked rifle and ready knife.

"Who guards the Lone Dove when the Bloodhound has left his kennel?" whispered Nehonesto.

"The Big Moccasin," was the captive's reply, and a second later he continued: "He and Nogawa know the Lone Dove's hiding-place. The Bloodhound would not tell his other braves."

On, on they went in silence, until young Somerville touched Nehonesto's arm.

"There's feet behind us," he whispered.

They listened.

"No," said the Ojibwa, at length, and the march beneath the wood was resumed.

All at once a groan penetrated the gloom the trio were piercing, and they became as marble statues.

Instantly Nogawa, the traitor, shrunk back, exclaiming:

"'Tis the Yellow Bloodhound!"

"Impossible!" said the scout. "I cut him to the death."

A second groan, more prolonged than the first, now reached their ears, and again they started forward. As they did so, the sound of footsteps in the gloom which they had traversed fell upon the Young Hunter's acute senses, and he was about to warn Nehonesto, when he thought of his first warning.

Presently a light greeted them, and they drew back from its glare to crouch in the shadow of the gigantic stalactites, hanging from the roof of the corridor.

Looking ahead with eager eyes, the trio beheld three figures occupying a dramatic position.

Upon the rocky floor of a large cavern, and opposite the mouth of the corridor, lay Jules Bardue, his head propped up by a bundle of furs. His cadaverous face was deathly pale, and his blood-shot eyes wandered about in their sockets like lost stars. His clothes were covered with blood, and it was Big Moccasin's unsurgical examination of the rent in his breast which had drawn forth the groans our friends had heard. Shrinking against the wall of the cavern, in the full light of the blaze, the spectators beheld Kate Blount, as beautiful as ever; but her face wore the hue of death, and the look which she cast upon the wounded renegade was tinged with triumph, while she trembled at the volley of oaths that rung from his lips.

"Nehonesto loves to hear the Bloodhound groan!" grinned the Ojibwa. "The Young Hunter did not reach his heart, but we must trap the dogs. Nehonesto wants to torture the Bloodhound."

"He is suffering enough now," said the scout. "Big Moccasin must be rummaging among his vitals."

A moment later the long-haired Ojibwa rose and stepped forward.

"Shoot them!" said Bob.

"No!" said the chief, sternly; and then he cried: "White and red dog, Nehonesto and his friends are in your kennel."

The startling announcement caused Big Moccasin to dart to his feet, and, despite his prostration, Jules Bardue followed his example, snatching a brand from the fire as he did so.

Then he staggered toward the captive girl, and suddenly paused over a piece of funnel-shaped bark, protruding from the junction of the wall and floor. The rim of the funnel was as large as that of a panama hat, and directly over it the renegade held his torch.

"Ha! ha!" he laughed, turning his hideous eyes upon the trio, who had pressed to the mouth of the cave and covered him with their rifles. "Shoot, if you dare! Though dead, I can blow you to atoms. I hold this torch over a lot of powder that communicates with a giant heap buried beneath us, and in a moment with Jules Bardue, the greatest devil that ever walked the earth, you'd be in eternity. Now, shoot, shoot if you dare!"

He laughed again, and the trio gazed upon him, transfixed with horror.

With throbless hearts they saw the torch blaze over the deadly composition, expecting each moment to be ushered into the presence of the stern Judge, for the separation of one spark from the flambeau, would seal the doom of all.

Instinctively Kate Blount shrunk from the desperate man, and in the center of the cavern stood Big Moccasin with folded arms, and stoical of countenance.

"What shall we do?" questioned the scout, fearfully.

What could they do?

Nehonesto was silent.

A footfall in the corridor broke the spell, and a moment later a quartette of rifles cracked.

Nehonesto's right hand dropped to his side, and Nogawa, the traitor, fell forward with a death groan. Bob Somerville, uninjured by the deadly pellets, turned, but ere he did so, he saw the renegade reel over the funnel of death, and, springing forward with a cry of horror, Kate Blount snatched the torch from his hand as it trembled on its descent into the powder!

Instantly the young scout saw who confronted him, and with the cry of "Kate!" he wheeled, and sprung toward the woman he loved.

He reached her side, and folded her to his heart in a loving embrace; but ere he could raise an arm to defend her, as he, with set teeth had determined to do, and that to the death, she was snatched from his embrace, and held from him by the snake-encircled arms of Coleola!

And he—he found himself griped by two red Titans, and, against the further wall of the cave, he saw Nehonesto being bound with strong sinews!

Then his heart sunk to immeasurable depths in his bosom, and when Coleola saw his look of despair, a devilish shriek of triumph pealed from her throat.

CHAPTER X
ON THE TRAIL

Doc Bell the giant scout was well versed in the geography of the Illinois. He had tramped that vast country at the dead hours of darkness, and, whenever pursued by a foe, he knew where to hide himself from the foeman's keen eyes. He often boasted that he could secrete himself in certain places, and rest securely there, while the combined tribes of the North-west hunted with the vindictiveness and keenness of the wolf for his scalp.

Therefore, when he suddenly turned aside with Oliver Blount, as related in a preceding chapter, he knew exactly where he was going, and long before the gray light of dawn the twain found themselves in a cave almost directly beneath one of the bush fringed tributaries of the Mississippi.

"This cave is none of the best of hidin' places," said the Indian-hunter; "but it was the nearest, an' seein' you growin' weak, Oll, I thought best to take it fur the present. That bullet in yer thigh ar' goin' to trouble you somewhat."

The trader admitted the truth of the hunter's observation with a groan.

"My leg is getting stiff now," he said. "While I ran it did not bother me, but now, since exertion has ceased, it is going to make up for the past. Oh, if that accursed ball had missed its mark! Kate! Kate, my child, where are you?"

"Kate will turn up all right, Oll," said the hunter; "such a gal as she ar' not goin' to be harmed by such a dog as Jules Bardue. When she becomes his wife, look for cats and snakes to drop from the moon. They'll do it then, sartain. But don't go on about her; think of what I've said, and take matters calmly. There's a God, Oll Blount."

"A God! Yes, Doc, there's a God, and from this minute I'm going to leave all to Him. He has saved our lives, and He will certainly watch over Kate. Now, Doc, look at my hurt, and get me on my feet against night, for I want to snatch my child from the hound I once almost whipped to death."

"I tell you beforehand, Oll Blount, that you won't git out o' this hole to-night," replied the hunter, stooping to examine the trader's wound. "You must be quiet for a day or so, an' while you rest here, I'll hunt for Bob an' the gal."

Oliver Blount uttered a groan of disappointment, which admitted the truth of Doc's remarks, confirmed by an examination of his injuries. The series of actions that followed the shot had irritated the wound, and a serious look overspread the hunter's face when his eyes fell upon it.

"The army doctors would say you've got to die, Oll," said Bell, "but I don't say so. You've got the worst lookin' leg I ever did see—no, no, don't look at it—'twould make you sick. I guess you'll git along, but you'll be a cripple. There!" after a long silence. "I've fixed you as best I can. I'll stay with you till night, an' then— Hark! what was thet?"

The trader started from his pillow of green branches, and looked at the giant hunter, whose eyes were turned toward the gloomy mouth of a corridor, almost directly opposite the main entrance to the cave.

"I didn't hear any noise, Doc," said Blount, still gazing at the hunter, whose right hand had noiselessly lifted his rifle from the ground. "You must have been mistaken!"

The giant did not reply, but suddenly started forward. A moment later, however, he returned, leading a young girl by the hand.

"Look here, Oll," he cried, addressing the wounded trader, "this is what I heard a moment ago. Look at her. Snakes and lizards! ain't she a beauty! I wonder why she came here, who she is, an' what she wants."

"Ask her!" said Blount. "I have never seen her face before. She's not a Peoria."

"Nor a Kaskaskia or a Cahokia," replied the hunter, looking into the black eyes of the Indian beauty, who stood before them as immobile as a statue.

Her face told of immense suffering at no remote time, and her large eyes confirmed the silent story. She was richly clad for an Indian, and reminded the twain of the savage belles to be found in every aboriginal village.

"Girl," and the hunter's arm, which had dropped to his side, touched her faultless hand. "Girl, tell the pale-faces who you are."

A deathlike silence filled the cave after Doc Bell's words, for the red beauty spoke not. Her eyes were riveted upon the hunter's face, and not until he had addressed her again did she make motion or sign.

Then she shook her head, and put her fingers to her lips.

"What does she mean, Oll?" asked Bell, turning to the trader with a troubled expression.

"She must either be a mute, or the stubbornest Indian girl I ever saw," replied the trader. "Make her talk, Doc, or see what ails her."

Intent upon obeying his companion, the Hercules of the forest turned to the Indian girl again.

"Does the red girl hear what the pale hunter says?" he asked.

A nod answered his question.

"And why don't she answer him?"

The Indian's lips parted now, but not a word broke the silence; and as she stepped nearer the hunter, her mouth opened to its utmost capacity, and for a moment he gazed therein.

Then he started back with an expression of horror, and gazing into the trader's anxious face he cried:

"Great heavens! Blount, she's tongueless!"

An exclamation of genuine horror escaped Oliver Blount's throat.

"It's true as gospel!" said Bell, "an' more, her tongue has been freshly cut out."

For a moment the two men gazed with pity upon the tongueless creature that confronted them, and Blount was the first to speak.

"What motive could have prompted such a hellish deed?" he cried. "It surpasses all the cruelty I ever heard of. Doc, can't you tell what tribe she belongs to?"

At this the giant again approached the girl, and taking her hand gazed scrutinizingly into her face. Then he examined her hand, and when he dropped it, he said:

"She's a Delaware."

"And she's far from home, too," returned the trader. "She must have fallen in with some fugitive Peorias. Oh, God, I wish she could tell her story."

The hunter did not reply. He leaned upon his rifle and covered his eyes with his tawny hands. The trader knew that he was thinking deeply, for when he gave himself up wholly to reflection and study, he invariably assumed his present attitude. For several minutes the giant remained silent and when he raised his head it was to fasten his eyes upon the speechless Indian girl.

"Where's Swamp Oak?" he asked.

At the mention of the name the girl started forward, and griped his arm, while an expression of anxiety and fear overspread her face.

"Ha!" he said, glancing at Blount. "I have hit the right trail. I just happened to think of the girl Swamp Oak sneaked from the greasy Delawares a long time ago, an' I knew, too, thet thet very gal had enemies who would tear her tongue out, ef they got half a chance, an' so I thought: might not this gal be the one? If you don't b'lieve it now, Oll, you will d'rectly."

Then he confronted the mute once more.

"The red girl met her mother, eh?"

The maiden's eyes flashed with fire, as she nodded assent, and her hands clenched in vengeance.

"Don't you see, Oll? Her mother, that infernal Snake Queen, caught her, an' tore her tongue from her head. It won't go well with that she devil now if she stalks within range of Doc Bell's rifle. Curse me if I couldn't cram her heart down her throat, although I have sworn never to harm a woman. I'm afraid I'm goin' to break thet oath soon."

The terrible condition of the beautiful girl before him had raised the hunter's anger to the highest pitch attainable, and, as he clenched his hands, he fairly frothed at the mouth. When Doc Bell was mad, he was a terrible being, and for a minute he paced the floor of the cave swayed by the uncontrollable passion of anger.

"Girl," he said, halting very suddenly before the mute, "I'm goin' to hunt fur your mother, an' by Heaven I'm goin' to sarve her precisely as she sarved you. You must stay with my pale friend till I return, for he carries a red-skin's ball in his body, an' needs your nursin'. You will stay with 'im?"

The girl—Ulalah—nodded assent, and knelt beside Oliver Blount, asking with her eyes a thousand questions.

"I'm glad you've got some one to stay with you, Oll," continued Bell, addressing the trader. "Now only keep quiet for I'm goin' to bring Kate right here, an' then we'll see if we can't git to Fort Chartres."

The trader smiled joyously at this thought, but he could not obliterate the terrible doubtings which had within the last few hours traced deep furrows in his face.

The cave in which the trio had taken refuge from the sharp eyes of their foes, proved to be one of the several situated in the Illinois which the giant hunter had often visited, and among its gloomy recesses he had established a cache. To this, after speaking to the tongueless girl, he made his way, and soon returned to the fire with an iron kettle and several pieces of venison. A lot of this he divided between himself and the trader, while he converted a portion of the remainder into a broth for the victim of a mother's vengeance.

Ulalah's eyes thanked the big-hearted hunter a thousand times, and drank the broth with an avidity that told of long fasting.

The day passed away at length, and when Doc Bell returned from a reconnoissance beyond the cave, and declared his readiness to begin his hunt for his friends, and, may be too, for the she fiend, Ulalah griped the trader's rifle and sprung to her feet.

"What! girl, ain't you going to stay with Oll, as you promised to do?" cried the hunter gazing in amazement upon the passion ruled form that swayed before him like the wind beset sapling.

She shook her head, and gritted her teeth with determination.

"The white man may die," said Doc, calmly, gently touching the girl's arm, "an' then what would his Lone Dove do? Girl, you will stay with him, to bathe his brow when the fever comes, and to moisten his lips when they cry for water. I will not be long away; I'll be as swift as the lightning, an' God helpin' me as destructive, too! Yes, girl—poor tongueless gir' stay with the weak man till the hunter comes back."

His pleadings availed the hunter naught, for Ulalah shook her head more resolutely than ever, and brought her foot down with a firmness that said:

"No more words; I am going with you!"

Doc Bell read the action correctly.

"She won't listen to any thing, Oll," he said. "She wants to meet that mad mother ov hers, an' she's bound to go with me. I hate to leave you alone, but I've got to do it."

"Go, Doc—go. I can get along. Go and tear Kate from *him*!"

"Curse the girl—no, I won't curse her, either, for were I in her fix, I'd want to settle for my stolen tongue, myself. Good-by, Oll. I've fixed every thing handy for you—rifle, meat, ammunition and all. Something tells me—"

He suddenly paused and rose to his feet, leaving the sentence incomplete.

He was going to say that an inward monitor told him that they were never to meet in life again, but he would not sorrow the parting with such words.

"Come, girl," he suddenly cried, turning to the Indian. "If you must go, I'll take you; but God knows I wish you'd stay with Oll."

Ulalah started forward at the hunter's command, and a minute later the stricken trader was the sole occupant of the cave!

And as he saw them disappear, the terrible presentiment that they were never to meet again came over him; and the thought of his daughter's fate drew a groan from his heart.

Then in silence he lay in the weird light of the dying fire, wishing God-speed to the twain who were hastening through the forest, toward a spot already tragic in the eyes of the reader.

CHAPTER XI
WHAT HAPPENED IN A CAVE

It was far from Coleola's intention to leave the country when she parted in rage from the war-party on the banks of Cahokia Creek, as described in chapter sixth. She retraced her steps to the hunted Peoria's hidden home, where for many hours, like the jungle-tiger, she lay in wait for her prey. But that noble prey came not; some unseen power held Swamp Oak aloof from the snare, and, when tired of lying in ambush, the Snake Queen left the cave, and sought for the Yellow Bloodhound and his pale prisoners.

Between these two ferocious characters an inseparable gulf had ever rolled, and each succeeding year it grew wider.

For a long time the Bloodhound and Coleola had lived at knife-points, and even in times of peace had attempted each other's life.

She found Bardue's trail without any difficulty, for she was an expert trailer, and came up with her great enemy in his own cave, when the rifles of our friends covered his cowardly heart, and when he held the lives of all in his hands.

The Snake Queen did not comprehend the situation, else she would not have fired without sober second thought. She did not realize the danger she was in, and flushed with anger, hightened by the presence of those whom she hated with all the bitterness of a mad-woman's hatred, her rifle spoke the words of doom.

Well might Bob Somerville's heart sink into the slough of despair when he comprehended his hopeless situation—when he saw Kate in the gripe of the mad Snake Queen, and found himself bound.

"Ha! ha! ha!" laughed Coleola, fastening her baleful eyes upon the trader's daughter, whose cheeks had suddenly assumed the hue of the undriven snow. "The Lone Dove is Coleola's at last, and her mate with the long plumage is hers, too. Coleola and her braves saw the Ojibwas and the white Hunter creep along the willowed banks, and when they entered the bushes she followed, and lo! here she is. Yellow dog!" and tossing Kate

Blount to one of her giant followers, she turned abruptly upon the prostrate Frenchman, who was glaring at her like a tiger. "Ha! the yellow dog is in the folds of the Snake Queen, and they are going to squeeze him to death. The pale-faces will hear him yelp with pain, directly, and then they shall yelp themselves. Coleola's enemies are all here save one—Swamp Oak, the Peoria dog. Oh, if he were here, and oh, if there stood at his side the girl who has no tongue!"

A moment's silence followed Coleola's bitter words, and then one of the braves jerked the creole to his feet.

He was dragged across the cave and stood upright against the wall composed of very soft limestone rock. He made no effort to escape; he knew that his strength would accomplish nothing, but he glanced wistfully from the fire to the powder-funnel. Oh, if he were free a moment! How quickly would he spring to the fire and hurl a torch upon the explosive heap—thus, at one fell swoop, sending his enemies as well as himself to eternity.

Coleola saw his glance, and laughed fiendishly at his despair.

"The black dirt shall not become fire by the Yellow Bloodhound's claws," she cried. "Warriors, nail him to the stones!"

Jules Bardue groaned aloud at this announcement of his doom, and he saw the Snake Queen's Indians snap the steel ramrod belonging to Big Moccasin's musket, and approach him, griping the improvised nails and their tomahawks.

They were going to nail him to the soft rocks!

Then he knew the knife would be resorted to, and he would be flayed alive!

At the thought of such a terrible doom, his limbs quaked like aspen leaves, and that cowardice which always nestled in his heart now rose up and bubbled from his throat.

"Mercy! mercy! Coleola," he cried, his face as white as ashes. "Spare! and I will leave this country, never, never to return. Woman!—"

"Nail the white dog to the stones!" was the unpitying command that rudely interrupted the creole's pleadings. "To the hound's cries Coleola is deaf; she couldn't hear him were he to cry as loud as the great cataract far toward the big ice-seas." [2]

The renegade bit his lips till the blood trickled over his chin, and in silence he permitted the warriors to push him against the rock.

He shrieked like a dying fiend when the first stroke of the tomahawk drove the pointless nail into his palm, and each succeeding blow was followed by a like shriek, until Coleola sprung forward and choked him into silence.

Under the Snake Queen's gripe, and the pain occasioned by the nails, Jules Bardue lost his senses, and when he hung from the wall by both hands, Coleola stepped back and awaited the return of consciousness.

"The creole's doom is terrible, but just!" murmured young Somerville, who had witnessed the red-men's work in horrified silence, not knowing how soon he would be subjected to the same fearful torture. "I am doomed to some fearful death, but I can die more like a man than that dog gives promise of doing. For myself I care not, but for Kate yonder, I care much—all. I wonder where Doc is? Oh, if he knew that we were in the hands of that mad snake-woman, he'd hasten hither and with his own strong arm tear us from her. Freedom! freedom! Oh, were ye mine for one moment!"

As he uttered the exclamation, the young scout tugged at his bonds; but across the cave he saw the wish which had lately leaped from his heart traced upon Nehonesto's face.

While the Snake Queen waited for the return of consciousness to her great enemy, not a word was spoken.

Bob Somerville gazed into Kate Blount's face, and in her eyes saw hope encircled by despair. Her dark orbs twinkled, too, with terrible determination.

What did it mean?

Why should the girl hope when not a ray illumined the cavern—when a speedy and horrible doom stared her in the face with all the grinning horror it could assume?

She was not bound; but the arm of her jailer encircled her waist, and his fingers griped her arm like the jaws of a vise.

She saw the wish for freedom with the determination that accompanied it in her lover's eyes, and she seemed to be waiting for a certain moment.

Kate Blount was not the girl to submit tamely to doom. She resolved to make a desperate struggle for freedom, and a glance at Nehonesto and the scout told her that she would be ably seconded.

Their enemies numbered four—Coleola and three braves, and the trader's daughter felt confident of overcoming them by a sudden attack. She waited for the right moment.

At last a groan escaped the Yellow Bloodhound's lips, and he raised his head!

Coleola sprung toward him with a cry of joy.

Now the devil's work would begin.

Kate Blount noted this, and threw a look at her lover—a look which he understood, for he returned a slight nod, and Nehonesto also proclaimed himself ready to help, so soon as he was set at liberty.

The eyes of the Indians were fastened upon Coleola now, and the gripe of Kate's captor had suddenly, and to no little degree, relaxed.

The brave girl saw the opportunity, and seized it with a determination worthy the bravest of her sex.

With no cry she sprung from the Delaware's arms, snatching his scalping-knife from his girdle as she executed the movement.

The savage with a shriek started forward; but suddenly he was hurled backward by the young scout, whose bonds Kate had severed at a single stroke.

All now was confusion!

Coleola uttered a wild yell and darted toward the trader's daughter; but all at once a dark object shot upward from the floor of the cavern, and, despite her struggles, she found herself in the grip of Nehonesto. He tore the twin snakes from her neck, and before they could bury their fangs in his tawny arm, he hurled them into the fire, where they hissed like demons in the agonies of death.

The savage who had guarded our heroine received a death blow at the hands of the youthful scout, and another of Coleola's red followers dropped at the Yellow Bloodhound's imprisoned feet, wounded to the bitter end.

The third brave received reinforcements from the corridor which led to the river!

The Snake Queen had penetrated the willows with seven braves, four of whom she had left to guard the entrance, as she feared the return of the trader, Doc Bell, or the avenging lover, Swamp Oak.

Now a peculiar shriek from the third savage who followed Coleola to the cave caused the guards to leave their posts; and all at once, like a quartette of devils, they rushed into the cavern, just as victory was declaring for our friends.

Then the conflict was renewed again with tenfold fury.

Despite his arm which hung shattered at his side, Nehonesto caught a warrior, and hurled him against the wall of the cave, at the foot of which he sunk with a crushed skull.

Kate Blount, too, performed prodigies of valor. She stood with clubbed rifle before the Snake Queen, beating back the savages who tried to free the mad-woman.

Suddenly a brave kicked the fire hither and thither, and then the fight continued in the semi-gloom.

At length, tripping over a dead Delaware, Bob fell to the earth, and before he could rise, a tomahawk, hurled from a red-skin's hand, stretched him senseless and bleeding upon the stones again.

A moment later, as a firebrand caused brave Kate Blount to reel, three dusky forms darted from the corridor, and she heard yells of despair well from the throats of the now almost victorious savages. New and unexpected antagonists had appeared upon the scene of action, and when Kate had collected her scattered senses, she found herself in the arms of Doc Bell, the Indian-fighter!

"Well, now, we got hyar jist in time!" cried the giant, looking down into Kate's colorless face. "It ar' a good thing thet we heard ye fightin', fur ef ye hedn't made sech a racket, I guess we'd be a good piece from hyar now. This is the Bloodhound's kennel, eh, girl?"

"Yes," answered Kate.

"An' where might the yaller dog be?"

"Yonder, nailed to—"

Kate Blount interrupted herself with a blank stare, and an exclamation.

"Why, he's gone!"

Yes, the white rocks to which the renegade had been nailed exhibited all their wonted ghostliness, and the Yellow Bloodhound was nowhere to be seen!

"How did he git away ef he war nailed?" cried Doc Bell springing to his feet. "The spirits don't ginerally help such fellars. But he's gone—gone to come back to us ag'in some day. Yes, that devil is far from dead."

"No, he is not, Doc," said Bob, who had regained his senses, and was wiping the blood drawn by the tomahawk from his forehead. "I cut all around his heart with my knife. Coleola's ball entered his body, and her red devils drove a ramrod through his hands. He can't get over all that."

"Boy, did Coleola's bullet take 'im atween the eyes?" asked the giant hunter, anxiously.

"No."

"Then the yaller dog won't die. Ye know how I hacked him up once? Nothin' under heaven but a half ounce of lead atween the peepers will ever finish 'im. He'll turn up in a few days again, afore we call ourselves safe."

A brief examination told the victors how the bloodhound had effected his escape. Alone he could do nothing, but during the conflict Big Moccasin must have freed himself, and borne his master from the cave, for the giant guard too was missing.

I have said that two persons came to the rescue with Doc Bell.

The identity of one the reader can easily fix; the other was the hunted Peoria—the vengeful Swamp Oak.

The giant and his tongueless companion had encountered the young chief in the forest, not far from the Bloodhound's cave. Upon the night when Swamp Oak had saved the lives of the trader and the giant by shooting Segowatha's avenging son, he had followed the twain but had failed to overtake them. Still he searched the forest, but the storm that burst above the trees immediately after their escape, had completely obliterated their trail, thus baffling the young Indian.

The meeting in the forest, mentioned above, was, no doubt, the strangest that ever took place in America.

The young Peoria clasped Ulalah to his heart, but started back to find her silent.

He then called upon her to speak, but still silent, she took his hand and put it into her mouth.

He uttered a cry of horror, and then the hunter-giant told him all he knew about Ulalah's terrible misfortune.

The hunted lover listened in silence, and when he had finished, in the dim light of a star, Doc Bell saw the Indian's face grow black with rage.

Again he kissed Ulalah, whispered *"vengeance,"* and she replied by pressing his hand.

The revengeful pair did not see Coleola until the fight in the cave had entirely ended, and Ulalah was the first to recognize her mother.

With a guttural noise, she sprung to her lover's side and pointed to the apparition.

For a moment the Peoria could not believe his senses, but when they assured him that the object of his vengeance actually stood before him—when he heard Coleola laugh triumphantly as she glanced from him to her mutilated child—mutilated by her own mad hand—he shot toward her with uplifted knife.

A single bound brought him face to face with his mad red mother-in-law.

"In whose power is Coleola now?" he hissed. "Ay, into whose hands has she fallen? She has hunted long that she might stand within arm's-length of Swamp Oak, and she stands thus at last. She found the Peoria's cave, but first she found Swamp Oak's sister, whose face is almost like Ulalah's. She bore the Drooping Willow through the forests until she found the Peoria's cave; she entered it; she slew the Drooping Willow, and tore Ulalah's tongue from her head. When Swamp Oak returned with the Lone Dove," continued the Indian, glancing at Kate, "he found whom he thought to be his Ulalah. He caught her in his arms, and her decaying body drove his brain on fire. Then Coleola came, and he darted away. Ah! the Snake Queen could not catch the Peoria, and when he stopped he found that he bore Drooping Willow, not Ulalah. Vengeance then he swore, and vengeance now he will have. Ulalah."

The speechless girl sprung forward, and, with wild eyes and trembling knife, confronted her unnatural mother.

The Snake Queen faced her executioners with dignified mien, and upon her face still gleamed that devilish expression of triumph.

Without a word Swamp Oak released one of Coleola's hands, binding the other fast to her body. Then he pushed her against the rock to which she had lately nailed the Yellow Bloodhound, and placed her arm against it.

"Coleola shall see her limbs torn from her trunk," he hissed, "and then her tongue shall be plucked from her mouth even as she tore her child's away; and when she has seen all this, then shall her eyes fly from her head as the arrow flies from the Indian's bow. Ulalah, come—the tomahawk! This hand plucked out your tongue. Cut it off!"

A look of triumph flashed from the wronged girl's eyes, and she snatched from her lover's hand the tomahawk it extended.

A second later she darted toward her mother.

The tomahawk flew above her head, and in the twinkling of an eye it descended, severing Coleola's right arm a few inches above the hand!

A soul-piercing shriek followed the avenging blow.

The mad queen shot forward, despite Swamp Oak's strength, and it was a giant's.

He might as well have tried to hold a crazy rhinoceros.

Coleola darted toward the corridor in which the Bloodhound and Big Moccasin had undoubtedly disappeared.

Kate Blount stood in her way, and noticed that her left arm was free.

"Back, Kate!" yelled the young scout.

Our heroine needed no summons to spring from the demoness' path; but ere she could shrink away, the left arm encircled her body, and she found herself lifted from the ground.

She shrieked, as well she might.

Four brave men sprung forward to rescue her from the mad Snake Queen; but their hands closed on emptiness!

Coleola and her beautiful captive had eluded them!

[2] Niagara.

CHAPTER XII
HUNTING THE HUNTED

Doc Bell, the giant, headed the horrified quartette that sprung after Coleola.

He rushed down the dark corridor as fast as his strong limbs could carry him, and suddenly found himself submerged in a lake of Stygian water.

"Halt!" he shouted to those who had followed at his heels, and the trio paused on the brink of the liquid death as the hunter emerged therefrom.

"Here's a deuced pretty go, ain't it?" he cried. "What kind of a cave do you call this, anyhow? Git a light; we'll s'arch this place. We're not goin' to let that gal git clean away from us, not ef old Doc Bell knows himsel'."

Bob Somerville sprung back into the cavern, and soon reappeared with a torch, which threw a ghastly glare around upon the water.

"There hev been a boat moored hyar," said Bell, suddenly stooping and designating a certain spot with his finger. "But it's gone now: that's sartin, but who took it?"

"Coleola."

"No she didn't," replied the hunter, looking up into the young scout's face. "Ther Bloodhound an' Big Moccasin came hyar first, an' they vamosed in it. Coleola war forced to swim, then."

"Where could she swim to?" questioned Somerville, with eagerness.

"Where, but to the other side of this 'ere black water?"

"And where is the other side? I see nothing."

"I should reckon you didn't, boy," said the Indian-fighter. "But, I'm the fellar what's goin' to find out. Snakes! I wish that Indian gal's hatchet had missed Coleola's arm, and took her accursed throat."

As he uttered the last word he handed the torch to Nehonesto, and he and Swamp Oak stepped into the lazy water.

A moment later there sounded the plash of expert swimmers, and the twain soon disappeared from those whom they left on the bank. They swam side by side a long distance in silence, and almost simultaneously their feet struck earth.

Then they ceased swimming, and drew themselves up on a cold, stony bank.

Looking in the direction from whence they came, they saw the glimmer of a torch, so far away that it appeared like a little star, in the milkmaid's path.

"We've come a great distance, Swamp Oak," said the giant, touching the Indian's shoulder, in the Stygian gloom that surrounded them. "Coleola is more than a woman if she swam this far with one arm, an' the burden of a girl to weigh her down."

"Coleola is in league with Watchemenetoc," returned the Indian, the superstitious part of his nature gaining the ascendency. "But," and he gritted his teeth, "Swamp Oak will catch the hag when Watchemenetoc is far away. Then!"

In the gloom Doc Bell smiled at Swamp Oak's thirst for revenge, and turned from the water.

The bank extended a short distance back without interruption, when our adventurers brought up against a wall of rock, containing many gigantic indentations.

"Ef we had a light!" cried the hunter.

A light was soon found.

The rough walls were covered with a network of creepers, which no doubt had perished for lack of sunshine, for a ray of the life-giving planet never penetrated this place. The Peoria tore a quantity of the dry creepers from the wall, and wrapped them around his scalping-knife. Then he had recourse to the invaluable flints, and presently the knife was crowned by a bright, crackling blaze.

They resumed their search, and found that the indentations I have mentioned extended out a few feet into the wall, and they were on the eve of relinquishing the quest, when a startling "Ugh!" burst from the Peoria's throat.

The giant sprung toward him and found him holding the torch over a dark spot on the gray stone over which they had trod immediately after emerging from the water.

It was blood—blood freshly spilled.

"On the right trail at last," cried Bell, in a hoarse whisper. "We can track the she devil by her gore now."

A step further on revealed a second drop of blood, and presently they trailed the wounded person into an obscure corridor, which had hitherto escaped their eyes.

Doc Bell almost uttered a shout of triumph, as he sprung into the dark passage, for he would soon come up with the Snake Queen, and rescue Kate Blount from her vengeance.

The passage proved a tortuous one, but no corridors led from it, and at length the hunter felt a breath of air fan his cheeks. He paused and griped the Peoria's naked arm.

They listened, and heard the low sound of rushing water.

"Go on, hunter," said the red-skin. "We will trail the mad queen to the wood."

They proceeded again, and at length, emerging from the corridor, found themselves standing up to their knees in a narrow stream that boasted of perpendicular banks.

"Baffled!" said the Indian-hunter, biting his lips with chagrin. "I've trailed many a red-skin before, but I confess that I'm crawling out o' the little end ov the horn now. Back, Swamp Oak, back to our people in the cave."

The Indian turned with reluctance, for he would fain have hunted for Coleola in the forest above them. He believed she was at that hour threading its recesses, in the gray light of dawn which was beginning to make objects visible. But he was mistaken.

He said nothing when the hunter stepped upon the backward trail, and they hurried on in silence.

They had traveled a great distance under ground, and, when no glimmer greeted their eyes as they regained the edge of the black lake, an exclamation of surprise parted the hunter's lips.

"Whar are our friends!" he cried. "They promised to wait fur us whar we left 'em; but now they're gone."

"They may be there in the blackness," said Swamp Oak.

"No, they're not there," persisted Bell. "Ef they war they'd hev ther torch up so we could see whar to swim to. Suthin's happened to them; now mark my words, Injun."

A shade of paleness overspread Swamp Oak's face as the thought of peril to Ulalah crept to his heart, and he was about to rush into the water and solve the mystery, when the hunter's hand restrained him.

"Hist!" he whispered. "Ther devil's takin' a ride—ther devil an' some ov his imps."

As he spoke, he took the torch from the Indian's hands and noiselessly extinguished it.

As he did so, the noise of paddles assailed their ears.

A boat was abroad on the inky tide, and for the first time in many years, superstition reigned in the old hunter's heart. It was an admirable place for ghosts to float their specter barks, and sail with their phantom brides locked in their arms. Involuntarily Doc Bell shrunk from the water, and turned his eyes toward the plash of the ghoulish paddles.

Nearer and nearer came the craft, and though he could not see it, he knew when it was opposite the spot where they crouched.

All at once, voices came from the boat, and the hunter clutched the Peoria's arm.

"Curse you, faster, chief!" they heard a hollow voice say, in a tone of command. "Heavens! if I were stronger!"

"The watery track is dark," was the reply, which stamped the speaker an Indian.

"Faster, anyhow!" was the hollow and grated rejoinder. "The devil is guiding his own now, and you can not wander from the path. The girl will wake soon."

Doc Bell griped Swamp Oak's arm tighter than ever, as the last sentence came to their ears.

"The gal, Injun; those devils hev got Kate Blount!"

The Peoria did not reply.

He was thunderstruck.

The trader's daughter had been spirited away by the Snake Queen; but now she was in the hands of Big Moccasin and the hated and hunted Yellow Bloodhound.

Had fate guided the woman into the hands of those devils? Even so it seemed.

The boat seemed a long while passing their station, and it was not until the voices were dying away in the gloom, that Doc Bell recovered his firmness.

"Swamp Oak, we must outwit those devils," he said, in his old firmness of tone. "My mind kin scarcely hold all that hes happened to-night, much less b'lieve it. But come, we'll foller thet ghostly boat, an' when ther Bloodhound runs ashore he'll find somebody he won't be lookin' for."

They rose to their feet and glided down the bank of the subterranean lake, a short distance in the rear of the boat.

All at once a peculiar noise told them that the prow of the canoe had turned, and was making toward the shore, a short distance ahead.

"Be ready, Injun," whispered Doc Bell. "We've got the dogs now, an' the gal, too!"

Unsuspicious of danger, the occupants of the boat approached the shore at the very point where our friends, with drawn knives and determined visages, lay waiting to receive them.

"Land, at last!" they heard Jules Bardue say, with a breath of relief, as the boat struck the rocks. "Furies! what a long ride that was. Here, chief— here's the girl; no, take me out first. My legs are stiff, but once on shore, I can walk. Jules Bardue ain't dead yet; no, and he's not going to die while his enemies live. Be careful, Moccasin; don't touch my hands; broken ramrods hurt like a wolf's teeth."

He paused, for the giant chief was lifting him from the boat, and, strain their eyes as much as they could, the watchers of the debarkation could not distinguish the forms of the voyagers.

However, their voices disclosed their positions, and as Big Moccasin laid his living burden on the ground, Swamp Oak sprung upon him.

The chief uttered a cry of terror, and as he reeled under the strength of his antagonist, a keen blade shot into his breast, and he fell, with a death gurgle, into the water.

Swamp Oak's work of death was inaugurated and finished in less time than we have recorded it, and, like a lion, he turned to the spot where the helpless renegade lay!

The hunter had shunned the creole for the boat, intent upon saving our heroine.

He knew that Jules Bardue was too weak to resist, and after he had rescued Kate, he would finish one who had already cursed the earth too long with his loathsome presence.

He clutched the canoe as Big Moccasin touched the water, and quickly jerked it toward him, for, unmoored, it had drifted from the bank.

The next minute his long arm shot over the gunwale, and his fingers closed on Kate Blount's slender arm.

He lifted her from the craft, with a cry of delight; but ere he could gain his feet with his prize, a noise like the explosion of a thousand pounds of powder bewildered his senses, and, with the girl in his arms, he staggered back, bereft of consciousness!

The lake of darkness felt the unseen blow; its sleeping waters sprung into life, and rocked with a hissing noise in their little basin.

For many minutes three forms lay motionless in the gloom, and at last the uplifting of a head was followed by a voice.

"Almighty Heavens! what did that mean?"

It was Doc Bell who spoke.

"Ten thousand earthquakes must have combined in one big bu'st; an' it war a big one, too. Kate!"

He shook the girl, who still lay in his arms, and heard her voice.

"Yer alive, thank God!" he ejaculated, with fervor. "Warn't thet a noise? Whar's Swamp Oak?"

"Here, hunter; his head is full of sounds yet. A hundred rivers rush through his brain."

"I should reckon they do. Did ye finish ther yaller dog?"

"Swamp Oak's knife was raised when Watchemenetoc spoke, and snatched him from the Peoria."

"What! did he git away erg'in?"

"He is gone, white hunter."

"It beats the Jews!" exclaimed Bell. "That dog bears a charmed life. Ain't he nowheres about, Injun?"

"No."

"The shock must hev thrown him somewheres. That shock! it cracked every bone in my body. I know what it war now. Somebody dropped fire inter ther Bloodhound's funnel, an' blow'd his cave to shivers. But our people—whar war they?"

A groan burst from Swamp Oak's lips.

"Where is Swamp Oak's tongueless bride?" he cried, in agony; and when the hunter thought where he left our friends with injunctions to await his return, a cold shiver shot over his frame, and he feared that the future would confirm the horrible belief which had taken possession of his mind.

"Come, Injun," he said to Swamp Oak, "we'll go back, now;" and he added, in a lower tone—"go back an' look fur their bodies!"

CHAPTER XIII
THE INFERNAL COMPACT

With Kate Blount, the sturdy old scout and Swamp Oak finally made their way out of that gloomy world, now made doubly horrible by the tremendous explosion which they believed had sent all their friends to their destruction. This belief Doc Bell had to impart to his fair charge, and she was terribly shocked over the thought of her lover's presumed awful fate.

But they were not to reach the cave, where Blount was left, without trouble. A careful reconnoissance by the old Indian-fighter revealed the presence of nineteen Ojibwas in the woods, right over the exit from the corridor leading from the lake. This compelled the trio to remain under close cover until nightfall should make it safe to travel.

In the quiet of their secure retreat, Kate related her adventures with the terrible Snake Queen, and how in the darkness the old hag had been stricken down by some unknown hand, but which she now learned was that of Jules Bardue, who, with Big Moccasin, bore her away. She had then become unconscious, and knew no more until aroused by Doc Bell's touch.

That the Snake Queen was dead Doc did not believe, but no time was given for further speculation, for Swamp Oak reported some one coming up-stream in a canoe. Doc was too amazed to speak, for in that canoe sat John Williamson! Had he not flung the wretch into the very midst of the savages, and how could he have escaped his doom?

No time was offered for questioning, for, discovering the opening in the hill, the haunted man, with almost a cry of gladness, turned the prow of his canoe into the opening and sprung ashore. The trio crouched back in the darkness, and John plunged down the corridor, as if to escape the light forever; and when the shades of night darkened the woods the three hastened from their cover to reach the cave where Blount had been left.

"Now fur yer father, gal," said Bell, addressing Kate, as they gained the forest above the creek. "We'll hurry up, fur I know ther old man ar' anxious to see his gal, an' she's sorter anxious to see him, too."

They traversed the forest at a rapid gait. Doc Bell knew the way, and he could trail as well beneath the stars as the sun.

A number of miles had been traversed, when several rifle-shots saluted their ears.

Doc Bell halted.

Crack! crack! crack!

"By my soul! there's bloody work goin' on at ther cave!" he cried, suddenly starting forward. "I heard Oll's rifle jest then, an' I b'lieve he's got help; but who on airth kin it be? Hold out, old man, till we git to yer! Hold out, I say. Doc Bell's comin', an' he's worth er stone wall an' ten cannon!"

The hunter ran at his utmost speed, and Kate Blount and Swamp Oak kept at his side. At length the yells of infuriated Indians made the night hideous, and drowned the crack of the death-dealing rifles.

"I knowed it! I knowed it!" cried Doc Bell. "Bloody work's goin' on hyar, an' I've been sp'ilin' fur a fight. Now look to yer rifles fur the last time!"

Creeping forward they beheld at least forty savages grouped at some distance before the mouth of the cave. These Indians were listening to the harangue of a tall chief, standing in the broad glare of the fire which they had kindled near the aperture.

Stretched upon the ground, as motionless as stricken statues, lay seven warriors, who had fallen beneath the rifles of the besieged, and the chief was firing the hearts of the savages, who seemed inclined to relinquish the conflict.

"Shall the hunted dogs drive the hunters from their kennel?" he cried, "and shall Segowatha sleep unavenged? The pale dog whose she whelp slew our great chief is in our power, if we but stretch forth our hands and take him. And those who fight with him are enemies to Pontiac's red war-dogs. Warriors, will you be squaws? Shall Tall Hickory go back to his people and say his men slunk like whipped hounds from a hole in the ground?"

The close of the speech had the desired effect; a chorus of hideous yells followed it, and the red demons demanded to be led once more to the conflict.

"Ready," whispered Doc Bell, with his eyes fastened upon the red avengers. "If they rush into ther cave in a body we must foller suit. Ha! there they go—determined to do or die, an' I calkilate some on 'em will die."

Unmindful of the doom that surely awaited him, Tall Hickory threw himself before the mad warriors and sprung toward the gaping mouth of the cave. He reached it, when the muffled reports of two rifles broke the suspense, and with a yell he reeled from the death-opening.

"Now let them hev it!" cried Bell, and a second later three rifles cracked.

A trio of Indians tottered against their fellows, and, ere they could touch the ground, the giant hunter was dashing toward the besiegers with uplifted rifle.

"I'm hyar! ye red devils, I am!" he yelled. "Hyar's Doc Bell what's sp'ilin' fur a fight; an' now let 'im hev a fair shake."

The Indians turned upon the mad hunter with a yell, and the next instant his heavy rifle stretched a Miami on the sward, while others were shrinking from the second blow.

"Back! back!" he yelled. "I'm yer master, I am. I've whipped ye on the Miami, an' I kin whip ye hyar. There! *you'll* never chase buffler ag'in!"

He rained his blows right and left, and beside him, ably seconding his death-work, fought Kate Blount and the young Peoria. The trader's daughter resembled some queen of tragedy. Her long tresses had escaped from the backwoods comb, and streamed down her back in wanton abandon, as her body swayed to and fro under the blows she delivered with clubbed rifle.

The savages soon recovered the equilibrium lost by the trio's unexpected attack, and, with thinned ranks, but more infuriated than ever, returned to the combat, and hemmed our friends in on all sides.

"Fight like catamounts!" yelled giant Doc Bell, above the din of battle, as he hurled a savage, who was about to fell the brave girl, to the earth. "Snakes an' lizards, but this is a tight place; but they can't whip us—never!"

The savages felt certain of victory, for their faces were flushed with anticipated triumph, and they contracted their ranks and rushed upon the defiant trio with deafening yells.

But suddenly three forms sprung from the mouth of the cave, and the Indians discovered that they possessed a trio of new antagonists!

Bob Somerville, Nehonesto, and Ulalah had joined our friends, and before the six at last the red-skins gave way!

"Boy!" cried Bell, springing to his protege, and grasping his hand, "I thought ye war a ghost when ye darted from ther cave, but thank fortin' ye're flesh an' blood! We thought ye an' Nehonesto an' thet dumb gal war blow'd all to pieces in ther cave."

"Ours was a narrow escape from death, Doc," said our hero, as a perceptible shudder swept his frame, "and I am much surprised to see you here. We waited for yourself and Swamp Oak a long time by the black lake, and at last reluctantly reached the conclusion that you had lost your lives through the accursed machinations of Coleola or the Bloodhound. Then we hurried from the cave, and had scarcely reached the forest when a deafening noise assailed and hurled us to the ground, bereft of consciousness. Ulalah led us hither, and after we had greeted Blount, we found that the accursed fiends had trailed us. How they managed to do so, I can not conceive; but they flocked hither like vultures to a carrion feast, and for several hours we fought more like demons than human creatures."

"And how is Blount?" questioned Bell, eagerly.

"Dying, poor fellow!" said our hero, with a sigh. "He's paid dearly for his stubbornness. But let us hasten to him. Kate should close his eyes."

Doc Bell turned to the cave.

"It's no use," he said. "Oll's dead; when I left 'im somethin' told me that I would never see 'im erlive ag'in; an' it hasn't lied."

Kate Blount was eager to greet her parent, and with her hand clasped in that of her lover, she descended into the cavern.

During the descent, Bob had told her that her father had received a severe wound from a stray ball, during the siege, and bade her prepare for the worst.

Reaching the bottom of the cavern, her eye caught sight of a figure lying in the light of the fire, and with a cry of joy she sprung forward.

"Father!" she cried, bending over the loved form. "Father, speak! 'Tis I, your pet—your Kate!"

Oliver Blount heard the voice, and opened his dying eyes spasmodically.

Then he tried to clasp her to his heart, but failed; his arms fell powerless at his side, and, as he gasped her beloved name, his orbs closed again, and a long-drawn breath told the trader's child that she was an orphan!

"I know'd it—I know'd it!" murmured Doc Bell, approaching, and dropping a tear over the weeping girl. "When Doc Bell's heart talks, it never lies."

Then he slowly turned to Somerville and the two chiefs.

"We are not out o' ther woods yit," he said. "I tell yer, it's a long way to Fort Chartres, and it ar' a black way, too."

"Full of fires," said Swamp Oak.

"An' dull knives," added Doc Bell.

"But we'll get there," said our hero, confidently.

"Not without bloodshed; we've got to see Coleola an' ther Bloodhound ag'in."

"You don't mean it, Doc," said Somerville, glancing at the woman he loved, while a chill crept to his heart.

He thought of peril for her, not for himself.

"I do mean it, Bob. Them two demons ain't dead yit, mind I tell yer. We'll see 'em ag'in afore we git out o' these woods, or my name's not Doc Bell."

"Heaven forefend," returned our hero, fervently. "I had hoped, for Kate's sake, that they were dead."

The giant did not reply, but looked to the priming of his rifle, and walked to the mouth of the cave.

"Halt! White Snake!"

A yell of horror pierced the almost palpable gloom, that brooded everywhere, and a groan quickly followed.

"For Heaven's sake, spare this life of mine! Mercy! mercy! I don't want to die now—no, no. I'm not fit to stand before the Great Judge to-day. Spare! spare! for the love of life!"

The words were couched in the most abject accents, and the teeth of the unseen speaker chattered like dice in the silence that followed the utterance of the last.

"I'm going to spare you, dog!" hissed a voice, so near the coward that he instinctively shrunk away. "I mean that I'll spare you on one condition."

"Name it—quick, for mercy's sake!"

"You must do my bidding."

"Whatever it be, I'll do it—only let one live who is not prepared to die. Who are you?"

"Jules Bardue—the Yellow Bloodhound of the Ojibwas," was the reply. "I do not ask your name—I know it. You are the most wretched man in these forests—John Williamson, Pontiac's murderer."

"Yes, God has cursed me with that name!" groaned the haunted trader.

A minute's silence followed.

"I am hurt," said Bardue, at last, "and you must carry me to the woods, when night comes. I dare not seek the forest now. In the gloom I can, by signals, bring trusty red people to my side."

"But me?" groaned the haunted trader, from the depths of his craven heart. "They will torture me when they know who I am."

"Only do my bidding, and they shall not harm you," said Bardue, quickly. "I rule the savage hearts. Oh, now the hour of vengeance is at hand. They have stabbed Jules Bardue; they have shot him; they have nailed him to a rock; but the Yellow Bloodhound lives yet to bite. Here, John Williamson, stoop down and pick me up. I'll tell you where to carry me."

Tremblingly the miserable man obeyed, and the creole hoped that he would be strong enough to walk when he joined his red associates in the forest.

The trader bore the Bloodhound to a dark cavern, and soon a fire illumined the place.

Then, at the renegade's request, Williamson related the story of his flight and wanderings from the jaws of justice.

If ever a truly wretched man trod the dark paths of the forests of the Illinois, it was John Williamson, and when night came he supported the wounded renegade to the woods, illy lighted by the scintillations of the stars.

For a long time Jules Bardue signaled his braves, who he knew could not be far away; but no answering footsteps greeted their ears.

At length the distant crack of rifles was faintly heard, and they listened more intently than ever.

The conflict at the cave was raging furiously, and as the twain listened they heard the deathly sounds die away.

"Williamson, we must hasten yonder," he cried. "Pick me up and run like lightning. If you do not obey, remember you're a dead man."

With an inward groan, the terror-stricken man lifted the renegade from the ground and started forward.

But his knees smote each other, and he feared that his burden was greater than he could bear.

He ran a few rods, and then, utterly exhausted, sunk to the earth.

It was in vain that the creole cursed his slave and in the midst of his anathemas a hasty footstep was heard approaching them.

The Bloodhound clutched his knife, but the next moment it was hurled from his hand.

"Ha! ha! ha!" laughed the new-comer. "Coleola and the Yellow Bloodhound have met again!"

The renegade groaned.

"Spare!" he hoarsely plead. "I will help Coleola slay her enemies."

The Snake Queen bent eagerly over him.

"Then the Queen of the Snakes and the Yellow Bloodhound bury the hatchet," she said. "She will help him eat up his enemies; he shall help her crush hers."

"I will, heaven help me! Where are they?"

"Below the ground," answered Coleola. "They have driven the braves before them like the strong wind blows the dead leaves away. We will kill the dogs. Can the Bloodhound walk?"

The sudden change in his fortunes drove Bardue to his feet.

"Walk?" he echoed. "I'm as strong now as ever. Lead the way, demoness. I've a blade that cries for blood."

Coleola laughed again, and, springing up, strode into the deeper gloom.

It was the strangest league ever formed in the Western wood.

Neither Coleola or Jules Bardue could accomplish their diabolical plans alone; so, throwing aside the bitter hate of years, they had crossed hands over the "bloody chasm," each resolving to massacre the other, when they had satiated the demon of revenge.

John Williamson, the haunted trader, went with them—never dreaming that he would soon cease to be a ghoul-chased man!

CHAPTER XIV
THE BITTER END

The giant hunter guarded the mouth of the cave alone until midnight.

He heard no noise save the voices of his friends below him, and the soughing of the forest trees. The ghostly sounds boded danger. The half-superstitious hunter had noted this, for years, and he was remarking it in a low tone when the cracking of a bough startled his trained senses.

Instantly he was on the alert, and presently his sharp eyes distinguished three dark bodies approaching the cave. They looked like panthers, but he knew at once that they were human beings.

Stepping back into the corridor he called Nehonesto, and the chief was soon at his side.

"Didn't I tell ye so?" he asked, looking into the Ojibwa's face in triumph.

"What does the white hunter mean?" questioned the savage in turn.

"Ye'll see d'rectly, chief," said Doc Bell; "they're after us, but we'll trap 'em. Back!"

He pushed the Indian into a natural niche in the wall of the corridor, and quickly followed him.

A minute later the mouth of the cavern was obscured by a black object, and they heard low voices.

"They are gone; curse the dogs!"

The voice was clothed in the deepest chagrin.

"But we will see!" returned another voice, which the hidden listeners at once recognized.

Then, once more, they saw the stars, but knew that a brace of human panthers were crawling down the corridor.

The third had been left to guard the orifice.

"We've got 'em now!" whispered Doc Bell to Nehonesto. "Ready?"

A guttural "Ugh" served as an affirmative reply, and Bill said:

"Chief, take the foremost, and, mind ye, hold the she-devil fast!"

A moment later the twain realized that the intruders were opposite them, and a low "Now" from the giant's lips impelled them forward.

Nehonesto's hands closed on Coleola, and Doc Bell threw the Yellow Bloodhound to the ground!

"I calkilate how a purty mess hez been spiled," laughed the hunter, in tones of triumph, and a cry drew our hero and Swamp Oak from the cavern.

"Here, Bob, hold this devil!" cried Bell, relinquishing the renegade to Somerville. "I want thet fellar what they left above us."

He sprung toward the mouth of the cave, where he stumbled over the crouching form of a man.

"Mercy!" groaned a trembling voice as the giant regained his feet.

"John Williamson!"

"Yes, but spare. Oh, spare!"

"Who said I war goin' to kill?" cried Bell. "I'm willin' to spare; but I'm desp'ratly afeard somebody else won't."

The trader groaned, and followed Bell back into the cave.

Coleola and Bardue had been conducted to the large chamber, where, sullen and silent, they stood before many an eye, flashing with vengeance of the direst nature.

"So ye thought we warn't hyar, eh?" said the big hunter, fastening his eyes upon the creole. "Wal, ef your red devils hadn't 'tacked this hole an' killed Oll Blount, ye wouldn't 'a' found us hyar, either. Ther folks war buryin' Oll when ye come, an' now I calkilate as how thar's goin' to be some more funerals. Woman," and he turned to the Snake Queen who was regarding Swamp Oak and her dumb daughter with flashing eyes, "how did you git out o' that cave!"

"Coleola crawled forth like the snake," she answered, suddenly finding her tongue. "The Big Moccasin struck her when she bore the Lone Dove through the darkness; but she crept away, and they did not hunt her long. The big noise filled her head with thunder, and when she opened her eyes she crawled into the woods. She saw the big hunter drive the red-man from the cave, and then she flew back to find the Delawares. But she met the Bloodhound in the woods, and they are here—Coleola and the Yellow one."

"An' what does Coleola expect?" asked the hunter.

She answered, quickly:

"Death!"

"Yes, Coleola shall step upon the death-trail!" cried Swamp Oak, darting forward. "She has torn Ulalah's tongue from her mouth, and Ulalah shall visit the same punishment upon the she-panther whom she once called mother."

The doomed woman uttered a terrible shriek, as the Indian halted before her with drawn knife, and when he commanded the avenging child to prepare for her horrible work, a whirlwind of passion swept across the Snake Queen's frame, and she wrenched her only hand from the thongs which held it captive.

The next instant she shot upon her daughter, and clutched her throat with the fiendishness of despair.

But, Swamp Oak darted to the rescue! He sprung upon the mad-woman; but was hurled against the wall of the cave by Ulalah, whom Coleola had suddenly transformed into her battle ax!

"Snakes an' lizards, what a devil!" cried Doc Bell, and he sprung at the Snake Queen, who was retreating toward the corridor, with the imperiled girl describing fearful circles before her.

"Back!" yelled Coleola.

But the daring hunter would not obey.

He flung his rifle above his head, and the blow descended upon the arm of the infuriated woman. Ulalah, speechless, fell to the ground.

The Snake Queen reeled, but ere she struck the ground, Swamp Oak was upon her.

He thought not of slow torture then. He thought Ulalah dead, so motionless she lay on the floor of the cavern, and his knife sunk to the haft in the red-woman's bosom! Then, while she gasped for life, the reeking blade tore her tongue from her mouth, and he sprung aloft with a hideous yell of triumph!

The spectators shuddered at the awful sight; but they were soon called upon to witness other scenes.

Doc Bell turned to Jules Bardue as Swamp Oak bent over the woman he loved.

"You've got to die!" he said, sternly. "All dogs have their day."

The creole did not reply, but fiercely eyed the speaker.

"You've made the earth run with innocent blood," continued Doc, "an' hed it not been fur ye, he whom we just buried, would hev still been livin'. Hev ye got any thin' to say afore ye go?"

There was no reply, and the hunter turned to our friends.

"By whose hand shall the dog die?" he asked.

A painful silence followed, and at length the hunter stepped aside, and picked up a handful of small stones. He then turned to our hero:

"How many, Bob?"

"Twenty."

"What's yer guess, Swamp Oak?"

The Peoria indicated fifteen with his fingers, and Nehonesto twenty-five.

Slowly Bill opened his hand, saying "Twenty-two" as he did so. A careful count told that he had guessed the exact number of the pebbles!

"I knowed it war to be thus," he said, slowly, and stepped back looking to the priming of his rifle.

Jules Bardue faced him with pallid countenance, and wildly beating heart!

He knew that the end of his bloody life was at hand.

The spectators shrunk from the doomed man, and turned their eyes upon his executioner.

For a moment the hunter's eyes glanced along the polished barrel, and then a jet of fire leaped from the bore.

The Yellow Bloodhound shrieked, and dropped to the ground—stone-dead!

"I told ye that nothin' but a bullet atween the eyes would finish 'im," said Doc Bell, turning to the spectators, "an' he's got it at last!"

For a moment silence reigned, and then the cry of "Mercy" echoed throughout the cavern.

It came from John Williamson's throat, and Bob Somerville sprung forward to save him from the Peoria's vengeance.

But he was too late!

He saw the Indian's knife dart toward the trader's breast, and when he touched the bare red arm, the knife, reeking with blood, had been withdrawn.

"Through him has Swamp Oak's relatives fallen," said the savage, releasing the corpse. "He killed Pontiac; he brought the torch and scalping-knife to the forests of the Illinois; and the squaws and pappooses of the Peorias fall before the red dogs as fast as the rain falls from the black clouds. Now the demons of the dark land will chase the pale-face no longer."

"Now for Fort Chartres!" said Bell. "We mought as well start at once, fur it's er long journey, an' ther way is black with death. But I think we've hed enough ov scrimmages to last er lifetime, an' I b'lieve thet God ar' a-goin' to keep us all safe now, till we see ther old fort erg'in. I want ter leave this kentry, an' git back to ther Miami. I'm used to ther lay ov thet land, an' they don't talk erbout skinnin' erlive thar, either."

A few minutes later the entire party left the cave, and stepped upon the long trail.

We need not follow them, for their journey would not interest the reader, who has followed their fortunes over the winding trail of death.

A mighty hand guided them through the new dangers, and at last the English flag rose upon their vision.

A cry of joy burst from the little band.

Now they could enjoy peace, for the last peril had been passed in safety, and they could thrill the hearts of others with a narration of their adventures.

A few days after the return to the fort, Bob Somerville called Kate Blount "wife," and after the interesting ceremony Doc Bell turned his face toward the death-regions of Ohio, where, in a forest drama, as startling as the one just penned, the reader shall encounter him again.

Ulalah remained in Fort Chartres till the close of the avengers' war, when Swamp Oak returned from the bloody forest-paths, and took his silent bird to a home far from the ruins of his tribe's wigwams.

Nehonesto followed Doc Bell to the valleys of the Miami.

And now, reader, the pen must be thrown aside again. But first, let me say that the mystery that enwraps the explosion of the Bloodhound's cave, and John Williamson's escape from the Indians on the Cahokia, remains to the humble writer a mystery still.

It may never be penetrated.

9 789364 287906